PRAISE FOR
NEIGHBORHOOD LINES

Neighborhood Lines is a must read. As a 29-year veteran of the Boston Police I have lived and worked in both of these neighborhoods. Michael has taken on a hot button topic and has brought it to print; a book that every high school should have on it's reading list. After reading it, children will rethink how they view people from different ethnic backgrounds. This book shows that true friendships are color blind.

DETECTIVE TIM STANTON BPD

A superbly written tale of two men; each from a different side of the tracks. Murphy shines a light on a dark subject and causes one to re-think their view of the world around them… a world that may be as close as their own neighborhood.

PAUL CARTER, SOUTH BOSTON

M.P. Murphy tells a powerful story of two boys in the neighborhoods of Boston, at a time when the color of your skin was the boundary line. A MUST READ!

KEVIN CHAPMAN, ACTOR, DORCHESTER

Neighborhood Lines tells a gripping and engaging story of America's struggles with race, culture and ethnicity. It's fitting that Nate and Patrick, two kids from opposing communities in Boston, can share their experiences as they come of age in a world full of challenges. *Neighborhood Lines* is an easy read that will leave you wanting more.

CORNELL MILLS, ROXBURY

Michael Murphy's book is a story right out of today's newspaper—breaking stereotypes and opening our minds to the beautiful possibility of what can happen when we look beyond the surface.

DAN PHILLIPS, PHILLIPS DIPISA CEO

Neighborhood Lines is a window into life in early 1990's Boston. Murphy has accurately portrayed the boundaries and personalities that made the city distinct in its tribalism at the time. The story's two main characters make for a compelling tale of adolescent rivalry, racial strife, and human frailty set upon the backdrop of a city that few would recognize today. Read this novel for a vivid trip to the old neighborhoods...and the subjects that remain topical today.

CHRIS MURRAY, ATTORNEY

I loved it. That period of time was swept under the carpet and has not been written about. It was such a weird, ugly period, but Murphy opens it up in a therapeutic way. And the timing is right!

JOE MALONE- FORMER MASSACHUSETTS STATE TREASURER AND
BOSTON RADIO AND TV PERSONALITY

Reading *Neighborhood Lines* was an emotional rollercoaster that captured me from beginning to end. Every element pulls you deeper into the character's feelings of loyalty, happiness, prejudice, and anger. Murphy's ability to balance character development with a detailed and captivating storyline transported me back into South Boston in 1990.

CHAD BOULAY, DIRECTOR, REAL ESTATE INVESTMENTS, BOSTON

Michael Patrick Murphy's *Neighborhood Lines* adds important color and nuance to a different Michael Patrick's classic, *All Souls*. In this re-telling of the story of 1990's Boston, Murphy portrays the trying times with honesty and compassion. For those Bostonians—black and white—who lived through those times, the story of Nate and Patrick is a reminder; and for those who did not, it is a revelation. This compact book is filled to the brim with a humanity lacking in our sociological and political treatments of adolescence and race. A must read.

DAVID HARRIS, DIRECTOR OF THE CHARLES HAMILTON HOUSTON
INSTITUTE FOR RACE AND JUSTICE AND HARVARD LAW LECTURER

A great story that resembles the trials and tribulations of the past, to teach great lessons to the youths of the future.

I read this book in two days. I instantly cared about the two main characters, Patrick and Nate. Their stories show how we can be, both the light and the darkness in other people's lives. There is no good guy -vs- the bad guy. There is just a human response to our circumstances and environment. We can be both hero and villain, depending upon our choices. Although racism was all around Patrick and Nate, these unlikely friends got past the superficial and dug deep. They made a difference in each other's lives. Their friendship changed them at their core!

NEIGHBORHOOD LINES

NEIGHBORHOOD
LINES

MICHAEL PATRICK MURPHY

BROOKLYN
BRIDGE
PUBLISHERS

Cover Art and Interior: Steven Plummer / SPBookDesign
Brooklyn Bridge Publishing

22431 Antonio Parkway, Suite B160-419

Rancho Santa Margarita, CA 92688
teamplayer@access-performance.com

This book was printed in the United States of America.

I dedicate this book to all the people who have impacted my life, whether positive or negative. You have inspired me to write this story. To the souls whose lives were lost along the way to violence, drugs, racial conflict, crime, and corruption—your life impacted my own to write this story.

And to my amazing grandmother—you were and still are, the true "Boss Lady".

FOREWORD BY
JAMES KEVIN MCPARTLAND

WE ARE ALL born with many gifts, and our life assignment is to uncover those gifts, and give them away. Sometimes our gifts are wrapped in such a way that can be likened to a set of boxes of decreasing size, placed one inside another. A gift inside of another gift, wrapped in yet another one. And it is not unusual to experience the uncovering of that first gift, or even the first few, to be a setback or a series of painful life events. Yet if we keep going, we find that inside that cascade of boxes is the ultimate gift—a life lesson.

Neighborhood Lines is Michael Patrick Murphy's first published book, and his way of giving away his own special gift for those who will receive it. I believe there are many more gifts to come from inside the soul of this peaceful warrior.

When I first met Michael, we were both attending a week long certification course that dove us deep into the disciplines and practical applications of neuroscience and life transformation. At the end of our time together, it seemed I was destined to continue my education through a shared limousine ride with Michael to Denver

International airport. Stimulated by the week of transformative growth (and potentially prompted by Michael's newfound awareness that I had published a book), Michael began to tell me his story. Captivated by the pictures Michael painted with words, the fifty-five minute ride to the airport seemed to arrive curbside at the departure hall in a mere fifteen minutes.

As fate would have it, there was more to exchange of our stories, more of the relationship we felt compelled to build, and more time needed to share. Looking back, it makes perfect sense to me why each of our flights happened to be delayed that day—it allowed us time to share a fantastic meal and the opportunity to dive deeper into each other's lives.

Michael left an impression on me when our lives crossed paths. He arrived at a time when I needed to be reminded of a lesson I may have forgotten. I could not have imagined then, that just a few short years later I would be writing the foreword to his first novel—a book that will light the torch of motivation for those looking to push past whatever has been holding them back in life.

Packed with powerful life lessons, *Neighborhood Lines* draws the parallel of an education earned on the streets with one that is learned in classrooms. The main characters, Nate and Patrick captivate the reader with connection and inspiration. Take nothing for granted. Work hard. Honor your family. Live by the code of loyalty. Stand up for your beliefs against all odds. These are the values that jumped out at me as I read this inspiring and thought-provoking tale. I felt as though I were right there in Cathedral High School, or on the streets of Dorchester and South Boston, and in those houses where the family and friends of Nate and Patrick navigated their daily lives.

Determined to touch people in a powerful way, Michael has taken a stimulating and enticing approach with *Neighborhood Lines*.

He has masterfully elevated the impact of inspiration by bringing his characters to life with an edgy storyline that will pull you in and make you feel you're right there. From Ashmont Street to Broadway, *Neighborhood Lines* will take you on a journey—one you can learn from, if you are open to the lesson.

Michael Patrick Murphy is living a future that he is creating with intention. He has a passion for life, is willing to take risks, and yet takes nothing for granted, as he knows we must earn it every day. His humility will impress those who meet him, as he relates to people from all walks of life equally and authentically.

Michael is an inspiring teacher, a faithful student, a successful businessman, a husband, a father, a brother, a son, and a loyal friend.

And now, he is an author.

Neighborhood Lines inspires me to improve upon my own work as a writer. I have no doubt that this is the beginning of a book series that holds the potential to be made into a feature film. Michael Murphy has done a phenomenal job of giving away his gifts through this compelling story. He is executing his life assignment, and doing so with excellence.

With gratitude,

Author of *Unopened Gifts*
Founder of Access Performance International

PREFACE

AS A CHILD growing up I paid an extreme amount of attention to what was going on in the world. From the adults around me to society as a whole, the war between good and evil, politics, history, news, sports and the streets.

My grandmother born and raised in South Boston, was the wife of a Boston Irish Catholic who was a World War II Navy deep-sea diver that stormed the beach on D-Day. She never let a moment pass without loving, laughing, sharing countless stories of her Boston Irish-American culture, and talking about politics. I became intrigued with her stories of JFK, James Michael Curley (a.k.a "the mayor of the poor"), John McCormack, and cardinal Cushing and of course her father.

My great-grandfather and his political associates had all been "cut from the same cloth" as she would say. He was one of the many Boston Irish politicians during the first half of the 1900's, who later became a superior court deputy sheriff at the statehouse. Legend has it that Mayor Curley had a few run-ins with the law, and so it was for his close associate my great-grandfather, Boston City Councilman Michael Mahoney. *(But they both would say "I' d do it again!")*.

I originally wrote *Neighborhood Lines* back in 1997 while taking a college writing class. I set out to capture a period of time in Boston-- between 1988 and 1995, tying in and intertwining the happenings of history throughout. Life was a rollercoaster at every turn as I had spent the past ten years getting an education on Morrissey Boulevard-- my high school and college years lived out in and around Dorchester, South Boston, and Boston. I spent many years working at various Boston union construction sites starting at the age of 14, gaining experiences that taught me a plethora of lessons for years to come. I remember feeling continually compelled and thinking to myself, "I have to write all this down".

Many incidents were fueled by racial feelings and fear during those years.

The imbedded, pre-established brain viruses and behavioral norms of the youth were clearly passed down through the realities, experiences, and truths of the adults within Boston's culture and society.

The two main characters of the story, Nate and Patrick, meet on each side of the racial lines, drawn by a newly implemented integration program at a longtime historic Boston Irish Catholic high school. The culture and society in which the students live, their ethnicities, families, and the neighborhoods of Boston are deeply portrayed throughout the tale. Tensions build between Nate and Patrick, as the relationship is continually challenged, limited, and inundated with interactions that bring waves of emotion—from love to hate, to fear, confusion, and anger.

With the increase of racial tension throughout America in the last several years, the urgency to publish *Neighborhood Lines* has been gnawing at me. The impact of the global political culture, terrorism, and random U.S. school, corporate and public shootings are brought right into our very homes, as the Internet has changed the world. In terms of information availability, the planet feels only a mile wide.

Life is changing so fast, I often find myself questioning: Are things worse now, or were they worse back then?

Some time in the late 90's, the landscape of Boston politics started to change for the better, and it was tangibly felt. Corruption was down, Whitey was gone, and the murder rate had dropped by fifty percent. The positive seeds of Mayor Flynn's policies had been taken over by a young Menino. He was making massive impacts, and major changes were taking place in the statehouse. Sports teams, businesses, unions, Cambridge, and Seaport—the last 20 years have been a great time to be alive in Boston! The time has gone by in a blink, and gentrification has been occurring to where certain areas of the city are now barely recognizable from the Boston I write about in *Neighborhood Lines*. The intent of telling this story of the past is to give voice to and shed light on the progress and lessons of race, power, and class—in hopes of bringing about continued, positive change in the future.

I have always strived to live, create, and write with passion. The experiences of my youth filled me with a strong desire to write about the stories of life, the different paths we take, and the people and crossroads we encounter along the way. Reflection of being a son and a father has impacted my soul in so many ways, life's endless lessons have no shortage of love, pain, accomplishments, and challenges. However, I now realize we often fail to see the abundance of the most amazing things in the present moment.

I hope this book makes you laugh, cry, ask important questions, and most of all *feel*. Breathe through your deepest wounds, darkest fears, and rawest of emotions. Allow your stories, culture, and life lessons to contribute to your greatness. May consciousness and awareness always be your guide to growth. Live in the present and focus on the now!

The process of bringing *Neighborhood Lines* to you has been so much fun. Stay tuned… there's more to come!

CHAPTER 1

Suffolk County Jail: May, 1991

"**Y**O, WHERE YOU goin, Prospect?"

Prospect's heart thumped in his chest like it was trying to escape his body. A wave of jeers and snickers echoed down the hall as a couple dozen young men in orange jumpsuits watched the two guards march him past their cells.

It was impossible to know who had asked the question, as Prospect's eyes were swollen almost completely shut, courtesy of his latest pummeling. He was being removed from the general population again, not because he'd misbehaved, but because the guards feared for his life. He'd put on a brave face—a thug face, he told himself—after his arrest, using every last ounce of his energy to make himself appear fearless. But the minute he'd been processed and put inside, they'd been able to smell the fear all over him.

And one whiff was all it took.

Day one, he thought they might name him "Preacher" when they caught sight of his tattoo: Romans 12:19, which a few of the inmates had recognized as a Bible verse. But it hadn't stuck, probably because he was so young. By day three, they had settled on Prospect. By week two, his real name, along with his "real" life, already seemed like a distant memory. For him, "Prospect" had now become bitterly ironic, a daily reminder of the death of his dreams. No matter who you were on the outside, in here, you started over at the bottom.

This was not how it was supposed to happen. He had had plans. Big plans. He was supposed to do more than anyone around him had ever accomplished. Now he wasn't sure if he would live to make it out.

CHAPTER 2

Boston, September 1990

NATE GRABBED THE brown paper bag off the counter where his mom always left it early in the morning before she went to work. He stuffed it in his backpack and ran out the door, but hesitated briefly on the steps of his apartment building.

The first day of junior year shouldn't have been a big deal. Nate would have started getting more homework and taking what passed for college prep classes at Dorchester High School, while a lot of his old friends continued worrying their mothers by staying out all hours of the night and coming home covered with bruises and cuts. The fights were sometimes just the result of adolescent restlessness, more often they were the symptoms of Boston's decade and a half social experiment with busing. Whites, blacks, Asians and Hispanics predictably stuck with and defended their own, no matter who they put in the desk next to you at school. You could integrate a social studies class, but the cafeteria remained as segregated as ever.

Nate's mom had had endless conversations with him about avoiding fights and gangs and sticking to basketball and his studies. "We've got big plans for you, young man," she always said. *We* meant her and Nate's dad, even though for years the remains of his body had been buried under a cross in Arlington National Cemetery.

And then in May, the letter had come. Nate was leaving Dorchester. Headmaster Father Lydon had announced a new program at Cathedral High School to take a hundred black students from the surrounding area and enroll them, almost tuition free. Grades, test scores and teacher recommendations were considered. Nate's mother had wept when she found out he had gotten accepted.

Nate hadn't wanted to go. Too weird and unfamiliar. It wasn't the geographical distance of Cathedral from his tiny apartment in Dorchester where he had lived his entire life. It was the fact that the immense brick edifice inhabited a different universe, with its nuns and priests and rowdy Irish and Italian kids, passing notes and sneaking cigarettes between classes. Nate could walk down a street in his neighborhood, or in nearby Roxbury, every day for a week and count the number of whites he saw on one hand. Cathedral stood in the South End, a rare patch of neutral ground between the invisible lines that divided all the city's dozens of distinct enclaves from one another. Roxbury on one side, then Irish South Boston, and on the other side was the legendary Combat Zone and Chinatown.

Those were lines Nate had never planned to cross, until today.

———

A few miles away, Patrick's mother was yelling at him to hurry up. He grabbed his Pop-Tart™ and raced out of the house, his backpack over one shoulder.

"This is total bullshit," his mother muttered as she started the car. "I don't even know why we're bothering to send you here. You might as well go to Southie for free if they're letting n*ggers into Cathedral." She took another drag off her cigarette, and Patrick thought she might cry.

"It's not that big of a deal, Ma," he offered, trying to calm her. The previous summer had been filled with almost nonstop adult chatter about the decision—rumored to have been funded by a handful of wealthy alums—to endow those extra scholarships. Father Lydon's explanation that the new students would take nothing away from the kids who were already there had done little to console them. True, Patrick's tuition was still mostly covered by a scholarship he received from the archdiocese. But it wasn't just about the money. "Look, Father Lydon explained it to me," he persisted. "They're just trying to give some of those underprivileged kids a chance."

"A chance? Are you kidding me? What about all the white kids from the projects in Old Colony and D Street? No one gave *them* a chance! No one gave *us* a chance, Paddy!" Ma was shaking with rage now, and Patrick was sorry he'd said anything. "Your great-great grandfather couldn't even get a job! No Irish Need Apply! Those signs were in every single window in the whole—"

"I know, Ma, I know!" Patrick interrupted, frustrated. "You've told me a million times."

"Then make it a million and one!" she snapped. "The point is, we had it just as bad as they did, but nobody lifted a finger to help us. We had to crawl up on our own, the rest of the world kicking us and spitting on us the entire way, and that's what we did. No one gave us scholarships or held conferences to solve our problems! And now a couple assholes who went to Cathedral and made it big want to tell me that my boy has to go to school with n*ggers?"

Patrick sighed. There was no use reasoning with her when she got like this. And he felt bad that they were paying money—even if it wasn't much—for him to go to Cathedral to avoid the chaos of the forcibly integrated public schools with their metal detectors and daily brawls. He wouldn't have cared if he went to Southie with his cousins and some of his other friends. But he liked Cathedral, and honestly, it was a hundred kids. What the hell was the big deal?

"Bye, Ma. Thanks for driving me," Patrick said, grabbing his backpack and slamming the door behind him and joining the swarm of students headed for the entrance. He was looking forward to his last year of high school, but had no idea what to expect from these new developments. "Slick!" he called out to a solidly built kid with dark, curly hair.

"Paddy! What up?" Slick called back, running over so they could enter the heavy double doors together. Inside, the halls buzzed with activity. Familiar figures greeted each other loudly, exchanging high fives and handshakes. Down the hall, just beyond a water fountain, Patrick saw four black students walking next to each other in complete silence.

"Senior year," Patrick sighed with satisfaction. "We're the big dogs now, man." The two boys found their new lockers and tried out the combinations that they had received in the mail. They had had lockers next to each other since ninth grade, since they were assigned alphabetically, but this time there was a locker between them.

"What the hell?" Slick asked, noticing the change.

"The new students," Patrick said, nodding at the locker that now

separated them. "You know, the black kids everyone's been t̶
about all summer."

"But this is the senior section," Slick protested. "I heard they w̶
only bringing in underclassmen. Who the hell would want to com.
to a new school just for a year, anyway?"

"Maybe they didn't have enough extra lockers in those sections,"
Patrick guessed. Another small crowd of black students passed them.
They were holding cards and looking for their lockers. Patrick locked
eyes with one of them, but neither of them said a word. "What do
you have first period?" he asked, turning back to Slick.

As the two boys discussed their schedules, a black student arrived
holding a card that matched the number of the locker between them.

"Can I help you?" Slick asked, blocking the locker with his thick
body. The newcomer was taller by about four inches, with a lean,
athletic build, and lighter by about 40 pounds.

"You wanna do this right here, on the first day?" the student asked,
dropping his backpack and walking right up to Slick so his eyes were
even with the new student's chin.

"Hey, be my guest," said Slick, thrown off by the new student's sudden
intensity. He slid to the left to let him by. Patrick was impressed. Slick
was a tough kid from Adams Corner in Dorchester, his parents were
off the boat. He'd only seen Slick back down like that a couple of times.
Once was freshman year when the two of them had been cornered by
four angry upper classmen because of a joke they'd overheard Slick
make. Patrick had been ready to fight—despite the near certainty of an
ass whooping—but Slick had had the sense to apologize. Something in
this student's demeanor had made Slick see sense again.

"Hey, don't mind this asshole," Patrick joked, motioning to Slick.
"Patrick." He offered the newcomer his hand.

"Nate," Nate said, shaking Patrick's hand firmly.

"Sorry, dude," Slick laughed, "Just kidding around. Later, Paddy."

and headed off to his English class on the
ng. The two boys assessed each other in silence.
class?" Patrick asked.

with O'Conner," Nate answered matter-of-factly,
locker and looking at his watch. The warning bell
ed. Boys up and down the hall began reflexively tucking their
shirttails into their pants. Nate's were already tucked in, and Patrick noticed his khaki uniform pants ironed so crisply the crease looked like the blade of an ax.

"Oh," Patrick answered, surprised. "Same here. You're only a junior, right?" He began walking toward Father O'Conner's classroom and Nate followed.

"Yeah. That was part of why my mom really wanted me to come here. Dorchester was running out of math classes for me to take."

"Gotcha," Patrick said. "Well, classes are tough here, but I'm sure you'll get used it." Nate stared at him a minute and then offered a nod and smile. Patrick couldn't be sure, but the smile felt fake. Nate said nothing more as the two of them entered the classroom and took their seats.

CHAPTER 3

THE CLASSROOM WAS already two thirds full when Patrick sat down at a desk toward the back. He saw Father O'Conner sitting at his desk in the front left corner, studying his notes; he had a friendly face with kind, blue eyes. The boys were whispering about how the police had already been called to Southie High School to investigate fresh vandalism—mostly standard, racial epithets that had appeared on one of the exterior walls before school even opened for the year. Everyone knew it was a waste of time to try to figure out who did it. In this town, there was no way anyone would break the code of silence and rat, whether the crime was murder or spray painting a racial slur on the side of the school.

Patrick watched Nate out of the corner of his eye as he took a seat in the second row and glanced around quickly. He was the only black student in the room. Nate imitated the rest of the boys as they dutifully put their hands together and bowed their heads, while Father Lydon's voice recited the morning prayers over the loudspeaker. Then to everyone's surprise, he continued to talk after the prayer was over.

"Now I know all our returning students are noticing some new faces around our hallways and in classrooms, in addition to our incoming freshmen. We are very excited about this new program t Cathedral and at our sister school, MRM-

orial High School. We expect all of you to give

varm welcome, and we look forward to what we

.ogether this year."

Conner moved to the front of the room, greeted the class

.ok attendance. "Welcome back, boys. We're going to start with

a little review," Father began, holding his open textbook in one hand and using his other to write on the board. His voice was loud, but gentle. "If I have a function, the f of x which is defined as x-squared plus one, what is the graph of this function going to look like?"

A few of the boys groaned as the reality of the new school year set in. That was the thing about having math first period—no essays on "What I did over summer vacation." Just back to work. While everyone else seemed to hesitate, Patrick's hand shot up. Father O'Conner motioned for him to respond.

"It's a parabola," Patrick answered confidently, laughing off the friendly jabs from his classmates, who were teasing him for being a teacher's pet.

"And where would the vertex be?" Father asked him.

"Zero, one," Patrick answered. More jabs, but Patrick didn't care. He liked math, even if he didn't always get A's. It sure beat reading boring literature or suffering through Spanish vocabulary quizzes.

Father nodded approvingly and asked, "Now who can tell me what the inverse function of the f of x would look like?"

The room was silent, except for the rustling of papers and the sound of students squirming in chairs. Patrick couldn't think of the answer. He remembered that they had learned about inverses last year. Something about flipping the x and the y. But he was drawing a blank on how to do it.

Slowly, Nate raised his hand. Father nodded for him to speak.

"There is no inverse function," Nate responded quietly. The room stayed silent as everyone watched Father O'Conner expectantly.

"That's right," Father answered. "And why is that?"

Nate answered, "Because if there are two x values for every y in the current function, then the inverse will yield two y values for every x. Any equation that does not yield a unique y value for every x in the domain is, by definition, not a function."

"Very good!" Father O'Conner answered, smiling with approval. "I couldn't have said it better myself. We'll talk a little later about restricting the range of the function, but let's move on for now." He wrote several more problems on the board, while the boys whispered and copied them down. Patrick was more than a little surprised. Everything he had heard about Dorchester High School made him think that it was a zoo, full of rowdy students who fought constantly and learned nothing all day. He stared at the back of Nate's neatly trimmed head, wondering how he could have possibly been able to answer the question so confidently.

First period ended and the rest of the day went much as Patrick would have expected. There were ten black students in his Physical Education class, but no one in the rest of his academic classes. He figured this was because his classes were almost exclusively with seniors, and no black seniors had been admitted. Nate being in his math class was clearly the exception to the rule.

He saw Nate again at the end of the day when he went to his locker.

"Good first day?" Patrick asked, dumping his books in his locker and slamming the door.

"No complaints," Nate said matter-of-factly. "You?"

"Oh, it was good," answered Patrick. "You know, senior year. One more year, and then college and all that."

"Oh." There was the faintest hint of surprise in Nate's voice. "Where are you trying to go?"

"Not sure yet," Patrick answered, caught a little off guard. He had had vague discussions with his mother and grandmother about college plans over the summer. They had talked about Boston College,

Boston University and Northeastern, but he couldn't remember what school they had actually decided on. All he knew was he was going.

"Well, it's good to apply to a lot of places, so then you have options," Nate said. Again that confidence—the same he had shown when he answered the question in math class. Patrick didn't know how to respond.

"Right," he answered. "Well, see you tomorrow."

"See ya," Nate called, shutting his locker and slinging his backpack over his shoulder. Patrick made his way toward the exit, when he caught sight of Father Lydon in the hall.

"Hey there, Patrick!" Father Lydon called out to him. "You in a rush to get home?"

"No, Father," Patrick responded warmly. Even when he had complained about the uniform, the extra homework, the strict priests, the lack of girls in his classes and all the other things that made Cathedral different from Southie, he had always liked Father Lydon. He was a Southie guy, born and raised. Even as a little boy sitting in Mass or practicing for his First Communion, Patrick had laughed at his jokes and found comfort in his gentle but frank demeanor. It had also been clear that Father Lydon looked out for him, especially after Patrick's father disappeared ten years ago. This might have made him or his mom uncomfortable if he'd been one of those priests who always seemed to be paying special attention to certain boys. But Father Lydon had always been above board in that regard.

"Come into my office and chat for a minute," Father said, motioning him to follow. Patrick obeyed, walking behind him until they reached his office. It wasn't a large room, but it was full of books. Behind the desk—which was covered with several of stacks of papers, a bulky computer monitor and keyboard in the corner—hung a large Celtic cross. Patrick took a seat in one of the two armchairs facing the desk.

"So how was the first day of your senior year, Patrick?" the priest asked, sitting down in the large chair under the cross.

"Good," Patrick answered. "It's nice to finally be on top, ya know?"

"Sure, sure," he agreed. "It's your turn to be in charge, it's true. How do you think the new students are fitting in?"

Patrick thought for a moment. "Well, it's hard for me to say. I met one of them today. And there were some in my PE class. Things seem to be going well, I guess." Patrick knew they were both thinking about the busing riots during the 1970s in response to the coerced integration of Boston's public school system—a move that forced many students, black and white, to attend schools far from their own neighborhood. There had been endless protests, and white teenagers had beaten up a prominent black lawyer outside City Hall in 1976.

Copyright Stanleyformanphotos.com, *The Soiling of Old Glory*, Pulitzer Prize 1977

Then (as Patrick's mom never stopped reminding him), black teenagers had retaliated by throwing rocks at a white mechanic. Outbursts of racial violence had continued since—including riots his mother had seen just blocks away from their house by the Old Colony projects—although things had seemed calmer of late. As of 1988 this resulted in many unhappy parents and residents as South Boston High School had a 37% black, 24% Hispanic, and a 27% white student ratio.

Busing was one thing, but recently this young black woman attorney from Dorchester, Wilkerson, representing the Boston NAACP, had just won a class action lawsuit. She took on the Boston Housing Authority for discrimination of public housing placement and violation of the Fair Housing Act of 1968. So the city had just begun integrating the all-white housing projects throughout South Boston and Charlestown. This just stirred up the neighborhood and the city all over again.

1988 WGBH News Report on Discrimination Lawsuit against Boston Housing Authority regarding integration of Housing projects.

Patrick thought back to the tense conversations between neighborhood adults all summer. He knew Cathedral's decision to integrate could cause the streets to explode again.

Boston Police officers flip a police cruiser back over after it was overturned by a crowd during a disturbance at South Boston High School on Dec. 11, 1974. A clash between the police and a crowd of 1500 people outside the school after a student was stabbed inside led to the closing of seven public schools in South Boston and Roxbury for the remainder of the week.

"Like I told you over the summer, I understand your mom and some of the other parents are pretty upset about this program," Father Lydon said, a hint of sadness in his voice.

"Well, yeah," Patrick admitted, shifting a little in his seat. "I mean, you know Ma. She just thinks all the new kids are bad news."

"I can understand that," Father Lydon, nodding. "Parents always want what's best for their children, particularly what feels the safest. And these are frightening times for people like your mom. Our city is changing."

"What do you mean?" Patrick asked. Ma was constantly saying Boston was changing too, but he had always assumed that older people just liked to complain that things were better when they were young.

"This is not the same city your mother grew up in. When she was a young girl, we Irish were the undisputed rulers of Boston. But that's not the case anymore." Patrick nodded and Father Lydon continued, "We've been here a long time, but we haven't been here forever. We came mostly in the middle of the 1800s. You've heard about that?"

"Sure," Patrick answered. Even Patrick's friends who had no idea where Ireland was had heard of the potato famine that brought hundreds of thousands of Irish to America.

"Yes, of course you do," Father Lydon said, smiling. "We came by the boatload, and honestly, no one was excited to have us. All of Boston was a wealthy, cultured city back then, and no one wanted a bunch of drunken Irish bastards stealing from their stores, catcalling their women and fighting in their streets, you know what I mean?"

Patrick laughed and nodded in agreement. He knew the history of Boston well, his grandmother told stories of the family emigration from Ireland all of the time. She grew up in the '30s and '40s, so she held different views than her daughter. She loved the Kennedy's with a passion. Bobby was her favorite, but she would always refer to JFK's book, *A Nation of Immigrants* regarding her father's arrival by boat in the Boston Harbor. She was proud of how her father had come over with a friend named Michael J. Quill. They had met as teenagers as members of an IRA Scout group. Quill had set up in New York and fought for human rights, started unions, and became friendly with Bobby Kennedy and MLK. She recalled Quill's words when referring to blacks, Jews, and racial equality: "We all arrived by boat, we eat different foods, sing and dance to different songs, however we do not have to love them or marry them, but we must respect and stand united with them for the good of us all." MLK said, "Quill was a man who spent his life ripping the chains of bondage off his fellow man. He sees people, not races". Patrick loved listening to her. She would always read the daily newspaper and tell him stories of the shenanigans and corruption of the past. Organized crime and politics always walked a thin, intertwined line in this city, she would say.

"But we kept coming and we wouldn't leave. We got married, and we had kids, and our kids got married and had kids and soon we had replaced a lot of the original people who lived here. There are some who say we colonized this city. Others say we invaded it. And for generations and generations—as long as people like your mother and your grandmother can remember—it's been ours. Do you see?"

"Sure," Patrick answered. He understood that part. The Celtic crosses displayed everywhere, the massive St. Patrick's Day Parade, even the multiple graffiti tributes to the IRA. Boston—South Boston anyway—was an Irish town through and through.

"But that's changing, Patrick. It's not changing because of the blacks any more than it's changing because of the Hispanics or the Chinese. Cities change. That's just how it goes. And change scares us the same way we scared the people who were here before we were."

"And like they scared the American Indians when they came?" Patrick asked with a smirk.

"Ha! Good point. That was a little more complicated, wasn't it? But you've got the idea. My job as headmaster is to make sure that this school serves our parish, and our parish is changing. Remember, we of the Society of Jesus are Men for Others, and we need young men like you who are willing to live that out. Do you understand what I'm saying?"

"I do," Patrick nodded. Change was inevitable, he thought, but that didn't mean it had to be bad.

CHAPTER 4

NATE TOSSED HIS backpack down on the couch and went to the kitchen. The entire apartment was little more than a room, with a tiny kitchen in one corner, a table and four chairs in another. A medium-sized window with a radiator under it overlooked the busy street below. The couch, facing the opposite wall, served to set off the living room, which had a rocking chair, a coffee table with an open Bible and a tiny television on a stand in the far corner. On top the TV was a framed photograph of a stern-faced, handsome man in a military uniform.

Nate poured himself a glass of milk and pulled out the large jar of peanut butter to make a sandwich on the wheat bread his mother insisted on buying instead of white. There were days when he thought he might prefer to go hungry rather than eat another peanut butter sandwich, but today was not one of them.

He picked up the phone on the wall and dialed a number.

"Can you tell Carmella that Nate is home?" he asked into the receiver.

Nate hung up the phone and sighed. He looked briefly across the living room at the TV, but no matter how much he wanted to turn it on he knew he couldn't. Besides the photograph staring at him, the meticulously clean apartment was a constant reminder of his mother's presence, even when she was away at work. Which she was for at least thirteen hours most days.

Nate sat down at the table and opened a large SAT prep book. He glanced at the clock above the door and began to work through some of the math practice problems. They were not difficult—mostly algebra 1 and geometry—but Mom was right. You forgot how to do even the simplest problems if you didn't practice.

The outside noise—cars, children playing, adults yelling and music from the occasional boom box—drifted up from the street, despite the closed windows. Nate was used to it; complete silence would have felt strange. He glanced up at the clock; 27 minutes had passed, which he decided was close enough to 30. He switched to the verbal section of the prep book, drilling himself on vocabulary words, analogies, and working through a reading comprehension passage. Finally the hour was over.

Nate closed the prep book, leaving his scrap paper out for evidence in case his mother returned home before he came back in. They had made an agreement at Christmas. An hour a day, five days a week, of SAT prep, until he took the test in October. If he did well enough, he would be done. If he needed to improve his score, they'd renegotiate. Basketball was plan A, but you never knew. You could break an ankle, miss a season. Plus, your brain would be with you for the rest of your life.

He rose from the table and walked through the tiny hallway with its three doors: the bathroom, and the two bedrooms, each barely big enough to hold a twin bed and a dresser. He entered the left one and retrieved his basketball from the side of his neatly made bed. Another Mom rule. Beds had to be made military style. Daddy was watching from heaven, she would joke, and he couldn't abide a messy bed.

Nate left his apartment, locked the door and ran down the stairs onto the street. He knew his mother would prefer he stay inside. Like many black mothers, she struggled constantly to balance her son's need for fresh air with his need to not be hassled by gangbangers or shot accidently in random crossfire. Nate worried less than she did. Dorchester and Roxbury were dangerous, but from what he had seen on the news about Los Angeles, things were even worse out there.

Nate's apartment building was four blocks from a small public park. As he walked, he nodded to his friend Rodney across the street, who nodded back as he barely touched the hand of a passing stranger. Nate knew it was a drug handoff. Rodney had recently started pushing for Castle Gate, which controlled a twelve-block radius, the second largest territory in Boston next to Whitey Bulger's crew and the almost mythological "Winter Hill Gang," so named by the *Boston Herald*.

Whitey had been slowly gaining the control of the city since he was a kid in the Southie projects and his return from his incarceration at Alcatraz in the mid '60s. And his crew was on another level. They dealt in a little of everything: gambling, extortion, loan sharking, kidnapping and drugs, and they had politicians—Whitey's brother Billy Bulger was the president of the Massachusetts Senate— cops and (some said) even the FBI in their pockets. Castle Gate was strictly crack, in that their closest competition was a fledgling Hispanic gang called the X-Men.

"Hey, you seen Tre?" An enormous man with a red, white and blue hoodie had sidled up silently and was practically on top of Nate. He looked familiar, but Nate couldn't place him.

"Naw, man," Nate said without flinching. The man nodded and kept walking. Tre was Nate's cousin, and Nate's answer had been true. He hadn't seen him in several days.

Although most kids in Nate's neighborhood felt pressured to join up with a gang at some point, everyone seemed to leave Nate alone. Partially it was because of his basketball skill, he had been the star point guard at Dorchester. Partially, it was because most people were terrified of his mother.

He thought about the first day at his new school, and especially about his math teacher, Father O'Conner, with his pale, sun-spotted face. How old was he? White people always ended up being younger than you thought they should be. Father O'Conner's blue eyes had had a tiny rim of pink around them; they reminded Nate of his friend's rabbit that had run away years ago. He shuddered and put the thought out of his mind.

Familiar graffiti marked the brick buildings he passed along his way, lots of Castle Gate signs, as well as the boilerplate black power fists. Frayed posters of New Edition—the most famous band to ever come out of Roxbury—adorned many of the windows, even though Bobby Brown was trying to go solo now. Nate paused for a moment, dribbling his ball in place when he noticed what looked like a fresh marking on the side of the Laundromat. "Norfolk Kings" was written in black and gray bubble letters. Nate stared uncomprehendingly for a moment and then moved on until he reached the park.

The park was little more than a large empty lot, half of which was dirt spotted with patches of grass, the other half was covered with cracked pavement. Every winter, the cracks grew with the freezing and thawing of the ice, until now you could sprain your ankle in one of them if you weren't careful. The grassy side supported a creaking swing set and a jungle gym, while the paved section had a basketball hoop with a rusty chain-link net at each end. There were a few children on the jungle gym and swings and small crowd of young men playing a disorganized game of ball on the pavement.

Nate motioned a greeting to the boys playing ball and moved to the far corner of the pavement. Quietly and methodically, he began his drills. Dribbling quickly with his right hand for about ten minutes, then with his left for even longer. Then between the legs. Then crossing over and all the different combinations he had learned at the summer camp his mother had saved to send him to. Then he was ready for his shooting drills.

Slugs, a huge figure who always reminded Nate of the titular character in the "Fat Albert" cartoon, saw him finish and called out, "You need the hoop, MJ?"

"Finish your game, Cuz" Nate called back. Slugs was Tre's younger brother. Slugs had always been the more lighthearted of the two, although neither had been the same since their older brother Troy died three years ago.

"Nah, we done," Slugs insisted. "C'mon kids. Make way for MJ. He gonna play for the Celtics one day and buy us all Jordans, right MJ?"

"We'll see," Nate laughed. "Just tryin to play in college some-where right now." The rest of the crowd retreated to the other hoop while Nate did his shooting drills. Some played half court, but many stopped to watch him. Nate felt the pressure of their eyes. Inside he knew that they were counting on him, in a way. He was the brainy act. The player with potential. He was the one who was destined to get out. Lots of kids got hassled for doing well in school or talking about college in anything but derisive terms. Nate was not entirely sure why they let him off the hook, but he guessed it was because he treated them with respect, because his cousin Slugs was the biggest kid on the street, and because they probably hoped he could take them with him somehow.

Nate finished his shooting drills and played pick-up with rest of the crew until the sun told him that his mom would be home any second. Then—as he would do every day until it got too dark to go out—he said goodbye to everyone and began to walk home. As he retraced his steps, he saw two uniformed police officers—one white and one black. He did not make eye contact, but as he passed them, the white officer called out to him.

"Yo, you pushing for Castle Gate out here?"

"No, officer," Nate said, meeting the officer's gaze and then looking down. His tone was even and polite, just as his mother had made him swear it would be in these situations.

"You sure about that?" the white officer demanded, taking two steps toward him.

"Yes, sir," Nate replied, using all his willpower to resist the urge to tell the officer to leave him the hell alone.

"I don't know, Isaac," the white cop said, shaking his head. "Let's check him out." Obediently, Nate followed the officer's instruction to turn toward the wall of the nearby building, putting his basketball down and spreading his hands and feet. The officer shoved him into wall, and then his hands went up and down Nate's legs, stopping an uncomfortably long time around his groin. Then he went into his pockets, up and down his torso, up and down his arms. He could feel and smell the cop's nasty breath on his neck, but Nate willed his breathing to stay calm, willed his body not to shake, willed himself not to shed a tear at his humiliation. He knew they probably had him confused with Rodney again; they were similar height and build. He also knew that they could easily plant a vial or two on him if he gave them attitude. So he did as he was told.

When the cop was done, Nate picked up his basketball, and waited to be dismissed.

"You have a good day, kid," the white cop said. The black cop said nothing. Nate walked the rest of the way home, taking deep breaths so his mother wouldn't see the incident written on his face. When he unlocked the apartment door, he smelled that dinner was already in the oven. She must have gotten home a little early, he thought.

"How's my Cathedral High School student?" Mom called out, rushing to give him a hug.

"Fine," Nate answered, receiving her embrace. She squeezed him tight and stood on her toes to kiss him on the neck. As always, she seemed reluctant to let him go, as if this hug might be their last. "I stink, Mom," he laughed, freeing himself from her grasp.

"I know, but you're still my baby," she insisted. "Go shower real quick. The chicken will be another few minutes."

Nate obeyed with a sigh. Life with Mom was highly regulated and seldom varied. He almost always cooperated. But sometimes, the four walls of the apartment felt like they were closing in on him, and he wanted to scream. In those moments, he wanted more than anything to break free from Mom's endless rules, run outside and do something truly impulsive and reckless: mouth off at a cop, chill with Rodney doing whatever he did at night, or just stay out at the court past dark. Then he would hear a siren or a car backfiring that sounded like it could be a gunshot, and he would return to reality. Mom was right. He had to play by all the rules; there was no margin of error for a kid like him.

Nate emerged from the shower and sat down at the table. His mom had already filled his plate with chicken, mashed potatoes and about a third more vegetables than he felt like eating. She always seemed to serve steamed broccoli these days, he noticed, saving her collards stewed with ham hock for special occasions.

Mom sat down and said grace. The two of them began to eat and discuss their days. Nate diligently answered all her questions about his school day, from the details of Father O'Conner's class to whether or not his uniform was comfortable. Then it was Nate's turn.

"How was work?"

"Oh, you know. The same," she answered, smiling. Nate knew Mom didn't like talking about work because she didn't want him feeling guilty. What was there to say about working 60 hours a week cleaning hotel rooms for minimum wage? She economized, stretching every dollar impossibly far. Of course she made sure he had the shoes he needed for basketball, and he knew she had some money put away. He also knew to conceal it, in case relatives came asking, which they always did.

"How about your class?" he asked. Nate's mom had been taking Saturday classes to get her teaching certification for what felt like forever. It wasn't easy when you could only do one class at a time, but he had never once heard her complain.

"It's going real well," she smiled, and then corrected herself. "Really well, I mean. I like this teacher. She knows how to explain things so you can understand them, you know? Now, when are basketball tryouts at Cathedral?"

"Not til November," Nate laughed. "It's football season now, Mom. You know that."

"The coach already knows about you, though, right?"

Nate shrugged. "Maybe. It's not a big deal. They're a smaller school, but their team did pretty well last year."

"Well, I'm sure he knows who you are. We just need to trust the Lord that you won't get hurt this season. Did you see Alvin and Tremont while you were out? Aunt Carol is worried they're getting mixed up with some bad kids."

"Just Alvin," Nate answered. Alvin was Slugs' real name. "Tre wasn't around. Alvin didn't look any different to me. I mean, they both act all hard, but they sure aren't with Castle Gate or anything like that. Aren't too many other real players around here, as far as I can tell." That answer seemed to satisfy his mom.

Nate finished his food. It tasted fine, as it always did, but like the peanut butter sandwich from earlier, there was something almost unbearably monotonous about it. Sometimes, the thought of living in Dorchester for another two years filled him with unbearable frustration. Other times, the thought of being anywhere else terrified him. Every time, he reminded himself that it didn't matter what he felt. He would get out. No one else in his family had gotten out yet, but he would.

"Mom," he said almost timidly after he had helped her clear and wash the dishes. "I only have a short paragraph to write for English and ten review problems for math. After I'm done, can I watch TV?"

She turned to him and sighed. "Just this once, and just for half an hour."

"Yes, ma'am," he smiled. And hurried to open his backpack and finish his homework.

CHAPTER 5

PATRICK TURNED ONTO his block and paused before walking up the steps of the duplex where he had lived since he was born. His street was full of modest homes that were built to hold anywhere from one to three families. Some had been renovated to keep up with the times, while others had fallen into various states of disrepair. Many dated all the way back to the late 1800s, when industrial workers and their families flooded into South Boston.

Around that time, the Boston streetcar service had been extended to the southern and eastern shores. This had made it easier for everyone to get around, but it had also brought the Polish and the Italians, who began to settle close to the already established Irish enclaves. No matter how hard you fought for something, there was always someone waiting to take it from you.

Patrick looked across the street and saw a girl walking up the steps of a single family home. Her strawberry blonde hair fell in ringlets over the starched uniform that barely hid the enticing curves of her body. Patrick wanted to call out to her, but restrained himself. He caught her eye, though, and she paused and waved to him. He had already decided to ask Kiley to the homecoming dance next month, and now he wondered if he could take her to the movies before then without Slick, PJ and the other boys giving him shit about it.

Patrick's relationship with Kiley had an oddly innocent quality to it. They'd lived across the street from each other for their entire lives. Kiley was two years younger, so Patrick—who'd had his share of semi-serious girlfriends over the years—had only begun to notice her about a year ago. This past summer, with its warm nights and late mornings, things had gone further. First kisses stolen at dusk, then a little more. Kiley's parents were strict, so it was all secret. But of course that only made it more exciting.

Patrick pushed open the door, which they never bothered to lock. The main floor of his house contained four rooms arranged around a staircase: the formal living room (which no one sat in) and the family room were in the front. The formal dining room (where no one ate) and the eat-in kitchen were in the back. The family room opened into the kitchen, so you could see the TV if you sat in the right seat at the table. Patrick stepped onto the shag carpet that covered the family room. The soft brown couch and chairs were beginning to wear, and the table—some sort of engineered wood with brass colored accents—was scratched and dented.

He had vague memories of this family room furniture set when it was brand new, his dad unloading it proudly from his truck and warning Patrick not to put his feet up on the table. Back then, payday brought surprise purchases occasionally. Other times it brought incessant arguments between his parents, complete with the smashed plates and broken bottles.

The weirdest thing about his dad disappearing had been that their day-to-day lives hadn't changed that much. If anything, life was more peaceful with Dad gone, and Patrick's sisters were too young to remember him being around at all. Patrick used to imagine that his dad was doing something secret—fighting for the IRA, maybe—and would return home when the time was right. But now he just tried not to think about him at all.

On the wall above the fireplace hung a picture of John F. Kennedy, thirty-fifth president of the United States, looking serene, handsome and eternally youthful. The portrait reminded Patrick that anything was possible, as long as you didn't give up on your dream. Before Kennedy, everyone had said there would never be a Catholic president, and certainly not an Irish Catholic. But he had proven them all wrong.

The Kennedys, Ma would remind him, were not any better than anybody else when they got started. Joe had been smart with money, investing in all sorts of things, and had amassed a fortune. Then he had thrown himself into his sons' political careers, and Jack had made it all the way to the top. An Irish kid from Boston, just like him.

Patrick had what it took to do the same, Ma would always remind him. He could be a state senator like Billy Bulger, or a congressman, or the current mayor of Boston, Ray Flynn, another born and raised South Boston guy. The sky was the limit. You just had to believe in yourself and not give up.

Mayor Ray Flynn and Senator Billy Bulger

Patrick ran upstairs, changed out of his uniform, and returned to the living room to turn on the TV. Ma's shift at the hospital was over at 7:00, so she wouldn't be home for a few hours. Everyone loved it when she worked late, since that meant unlimited TV, and McGoo's pizza for dinner. About ten minutes later, he heard the screen door rattle. His sisters were in sixth and seventh grade, they wouldn't be home until 4:00. He turned his head to the door and saw his younger cousin PJ.

"Yo, Paddy! What up? " PJ laughed. Patrick immediately noticed that his cousin was sporting a freshly blackened eye. PJ was slightly built, but strong; he was always smiling and never seemed to have a care in the world.

"What the hell happened to you?" Patrick asked. "It's only the first damn day!" PJ had always been a nice kid, but he could be too impulsive for his own good sometimes.

"This?" PJ laughed, pointing to the eye. "Nothing man. Some n*gger tried to step to me over my new kicks. He got a punch in before I threw him in a locker. Pretty nice though, right?" PJ motioned to his shoes. They were brand new Air Jordans.

"Jeez, where'd you get those?" Patrick asked. Patrick's mom was a nurse, so they could afford some luxuries now and then. But PJ's mom worked at the local convenience store part time and his dad was retired, although no one seemed to know exactly what job he had retired from.

"Oh a friend hooked me up," PJ said dismissively. "No big deal."

"Don't be stupid, PJ," Patrick warned seriously, wondering what friend PJ had that he didn't know. "Don't get yourself killed over some damn shoes."

"Well, what should I've done?" PJ asked almost innocently. "Just let the n*gger take em?"

"You know at least half those guys are packin. And definitely don't jump on the Ashmont train wearing those Jordans," Patrick suggested shaking his head. Just last week, gunshots had rung out at a subway stop, leaving three dead and six wounded. But PJ always seemed oblivious to danger. He looked at life as one long, hilarious joke, which made him fun to hang out with, but didn't necessarily bode well for his future.

"Ya gotta live a little Cuz," PJ laughed. "Carp-pay whatever. Remember that movie? Or from English class or something?"

"*Carpe diem*," Patrick explained. "It means seize the day. From *Dead Poet's Society*."

"Right! See, that's why you're going to be President one day, and then you can get me any job I want!" PJ laughed at the thought.

"Yeah right," Patrick laughed. He didn't really want to be president, but he did want to be something. There were days when high school had felt like it was lasting forever, and real life would never get started. But now that senior year had finally come, he had a gnawing feeling that there were some concrete things that needed to happen. Nate's comments about applying to lots of different colleges had reminded him that he would need to get started on that soon.

"You'll be something great, you'll see," PJ said confidently, switching the TV channel without asking. "So what's it like with n*ggers at your school now?"

"Can't really say," Patrick said. "Just one in my math class and a bunch in PE. I'm in all senior classes anyway, and they were all underclassmen."

"Well, that's good, huh? I guess they won't make much trouble in Catholic school," PJ speculated. After his mother's reaction that morning, Patrick saw no point in trying to share Father Lydon's wisdom about Boston changing, or suggest that maybe not all conflicts between the blacks and whites were started by blacks. The city had seen plenty of racial violence, and there was plenty of blame to go around. But PJ, like most of Patrick's friends, didn't necessarily see it that way.

The two sat in silence watching a rerun of "The A-Team", and PJ began to doze off. When the episode ended, Patrick heard the screen door open and shut; Shannon and Danielle had returned from school, their uniforms wrinkled but clean. Shannon ran up to PJ and hugged him, while Danielle, who saw herself as grown up now, merely acknowledged her brother and cousin and pulled an issue of *Seventeen Magazine* out of her of backpack.

"We get the TV first," Danielle informed him, switching the channel.

"Whatever," Patrick said. He and PJ vacated the living room and sat down at the kitchen table where they opened a bag of Doritos. A few minutes later the screen door rattled again.

"Hey, hey, how's everybody doing today?" Patrick would recognize Sean's almost comically loud voice anywhere. Sean was short—still just five foot six or so—but he was broad shouldered and worked hard to make sure his biceps bulged in his tight tee shirts. He was carrying a six-pack of Milwaukee's Best, and Patrick saw Walsh—lanky like PJ, but not nearly as strong—trailing close behind. Walsh was a senior at Southie with PJ. Sean had graduated two years ago, and worked part time as a busboy at The Quiet Man on West Broadway.

"Nice to see you lovely folks," Walsh said, tossing a Red Sox cap at PJ, which he must have left at school.

"Thanks, Ma," PJ joked, catching it and placing it on his head backwards. He never was very good at keeping track of his stuff.

"Hey, make sure that shit is out of my house before Ma gets home," Patrick cautioned them, motioning to the beer.

"Oh, we'll be gone long before Kathy gets back, trust me," Sean laughed. "The girls get the TV? Seriously?" he asked motioning toward the living room.

"Let them finish this episode. Then you can switch it," Walsh said reasonably. Sean rolled his eyes and opened a beer, the others did the same.

"No fair," Shannon protested from the other room.

"Be quiet, and I'll let you play with my Gameboy," Patrick offered. The four boys had known each other since birth. Walsh and PJ had brothers and sisters, but Sean was an only child and never understood how to negotiate for things. Except for Patrick going to Catholic school, they had spent most of their waking moments together, throwing rocks and playing stickball when they were little; more recently, playing basketball and street hockey.

"Full House" ended on TV, and the girls retrieved the Gameboy and went upstairs. The boys moved to the living room. Sean and PJ both lit cigarettes, as Sean opened a second beer. They watched "Yo MTV Raps" for a while, cracking jokes and complaining about school. At 5:00, Sean rose to go. He was cutting it close for the dinner shift as it was. Everyone else got ready to head down the park.

"Yo, PJ, you gonna help me out this weekend?" Sean asked on his way out the door. Patrick's ears pricked up, but he said nothing.

"Yeah, I got it. No problem," PJ answered without looking up from the TV. Patrick wondered what it was about, but didn't ask.

"Alright, then," Sean said approvingly. "Later, boys." The screen door clattered as he left.

CHAPTER 6

SEPTEMBER WENT BY faster than Nate thought it would. He adjusted to his new routine without much trouble, spending each weekday afternoon with his prep book, his basketball and his homework. Before he knew it, he was walking home from Dorchester High School on a sunny Saturday in mid-October.

"How did it go?" Mom's voice was bubbling over with excitement and anxiety as he came through the door.

"I think it went well. Pretty much what I expected. You know, it's definitely going to get cold tonight." Nate replied, trying to reassure her and change the subject at the same time. He wasn't lying. It had gone well. He had finished every section early and gone back and checked his work. He was confident about all but a small handful of the math questions and one or two of the verbal. And while he didn't share his mother's obsession with this test, he certainly hoped he did well enough to avoid taking it again.

"Well, good," she said, hugging him tight and kissing him on the cheek as she did every time he came in the apartment. "But if you're not happy with either score, you can take it again, you know. That's why you're taking it now, so you still have time to raise your score before you apply—"

"I know, Mom," Nate interrupted, trying to be patient. They had literally had this same discussion dozens of times over the past year and a half.

"What about tonight?" Mom asked.

"I'm going I guess," Nate sighed, the ambivalence in his voice obvious. "Derek and Andre are going, and Betina and the other girls from MRM will be there."

"Okay, that's fine," Mom agreed. "But be back by 11:30 and remember, if the cops catch you with troublemakers—"

"I know, Mom," Nate interrupted. "I know. They won't care if I'm guilty or not. Young black men get locked up or shot just for being in the wrong place at the wrong time." He repeated the last two sentences robotically.

"Look," Mom said almost apologetically, "I know you're sick of hearing it. I know I sound like a broken record. But you have to understand, you have no room for mistakes, son. White kids can mess up all they want, and their parents can hire fancy lawyers to get them out of it. You so much as stand downwind from someone messing up, and it's over for you. That's just how the world works, understand?"

"Yes, ma'am," Nate said dutifully.

"Hey, have fun at the dance, Nate," Mom smiled. "Just remember that other thing I always tell you."

"Don't worry, Mom," Nate laughed. "You know I'm not gonna mess with no white girl."

Patrick tried to push the morning's activities out of his mind and focus on his last homecoming dance in just a few hours. It was his first time taking the SAT and he had not known at all what to expect. He knew most of the math, but had been confused by the way the problems were set up. The rest of the questions had seemed weird and by the last two sections, he was just ready for it all to be over.

But he had been anticipating tonight for a long time. He was borrowing his mom's car, and he would be taking Kiley. The more he rolled it over in his mind, the more he was confident tonight was going to be the night. As far as Slick, PJ and everyone else were concerned, he and Kiley had been at it since summer. But in reality, Patrick hadn't wanted to rush her. She was younger and genuinely innocent. She was also more special to him than his previous girlfriends, most of whom had been older and more than happy to show him the ropes. So he'd been patient, and tonight he was pretty sure it would pay off.

Kiley met him out front. Between the dress—a pink gown with cap sleeves and sweetheart neckline that Patrick guessed would just barely get by the nuns enforcing the dress code—the makeup, and her mother's string of pearls around her neck, she had aged two years. Patrick wanted to kiss her right there, but he knew how girls could be when they spent all that time on their makeup. Instead, he whispered that she looked great, yelled goodbye to his mother and sisters and the two departed in the family's 1985 Ford Taurus.

The ride was short, and they were both pretty quiet. When they got to the school, the lights in the gym had been lowered and "Roni" pumped loudly from the speakers. A handful of nuns were circulating inside, making sure that couples didn't get too close, but most were experts at evading their glances. After they danced together to LL Cool J's "I Need Love", Kiley found some of her friends from MRM and Patrick located Slick near the back door.

"Where's everyone at?" Patrick asked him.

"Outside already," Slick nodded toward the door. As usual, some boys had gone out back to sneak beer and smoke cigarettes and blunts. Patrick planned to join them for a beer or two in a while, but not just yet. Slick continued, "So now our homecoming looks just like Southie's, huh?"

Patrick said nothing, but as his eyes scanned the gym he saw the crowd was dotted with black couples. Well of course it was, he thought. They go to school here now; what's the big deal? He noticed Nate dancing with a slender, bronze-skinned girl. She was average height, Patrick guessed, but she looked short dancing with Nate. When the song finished, the girl and a few of her friends congregated in the far corner. Patrick and Nate acknowledged one another with a nod.

To Patrick's surprise, Nate walked in their direction instead of joining the black kids on the other side of the gym. Then he saw Nate squat down and pick up a hair bow that must fallen out of his date's hair and been kicked to the side of the gym by accident.

"That your girl's?" Patrick inquired, looking at the bow.

"Something like that," Nate admitted with slight grin. "We've been knowing each other since grade school, you know? You here with that girl in pink?"

"Yeah, same deal," Patrick laughed. "You getting bored? Some boys got some cases and a few are smoking up outside."

"Well good for them," Nate answered. He didn't seem offended that Patrick had brought it up, but he didn't seem interested either.

"Not your thing?" Patrick asked. He had grown to respect Nate, but he was far from understanding him. Sometimes he acted like a 30-year-old in a teenager's body.

"Nope," Nate answered, shaking his head. "Even if it were, my mom would kill me. Totally not worth it."

"She still waits up for you?" Patrick was amazed at the thought. His mom was exhausted when she got home from work and was almost always asleep when he got home on the weekends, whether on the couch in front of the TV or upstairs in her room.

"Are you kidding?" Nate laughed. "She waits up for me and hugs me good and tight until she's smelled my hair, my skin and my clothes. One time my cousin had been smoking—cigarettes, okay? Not even reefer—and she beat my tail to an inch of my life because she smelled it on me. So like I said, not worth it."

Slowly, the mystery of what made Nate different from Patrick's general ideas about black people was beginning to fade. He couldn't picture what Nate's mom would look like, but he began to understand that she was the reason Nate knew all the answers in math, why he was careful to speak properly to the teachers, why his clothes were perfectly ironed, his hair impeccably cut, why he didn't bang, and why he had no tattoos, or at least none that anyone could see.

"Man, I'd die if my ma were that strict," Patrick offered sympathetically.

"Yeah, well ironically, I'd probably die if she weren't." Nate let his statement hang in the air, but before Patrick could respond, Nate pointed to the dance floor and exclaimed, "Oh shit!"

A brawl had broken out between black and white students in the middle of the gym, and without thinking, both Nate and Patrick rushed to break it up. Patrick pushed himself to the center of the knot, grabbed two of the white kids by their shirt collars and jerked them back hard enough that they lost their breath for a moment. Nate reached around one of the black kids from behind, pinning his arms to his sides and telling him firmly to calm down. By the time the nuns and priests rushed over, the tension had dissipated and the students were returning to their separate groups in various corners.

The music continued unabated; it was unclear if the DJ had even noticed what was going on.

Nate nodded to Patrick before he walked back across the gym and joined a group of black students. Patrick and Kiley met up again at the next slow song, swaying to the music and letting their bodies press together whenever the nuns' backs were turned. Patrick snuck out back to drink his beer, and then returned for a few more dances. Soon he was ready to leave; he and Kiley had conspired to take off a little early, so they'd have some extra time before her mom expected her home.

Patrick had just said bye to Slick, when he heard a loud whisper come from the back door.

"Patrick!!" It was PJ. What the hell was he doing at Cathedral's homecoming?

"Jesus, PJ, what are you doing here?" Patrick asked, moving toward the door. "If you wanted to come I could've got you a ticket," he added with a laugh.

"No, no, I don't want to come in," PJ said quickly, his voice agitated.

"What is it?" Suddenly, Patrick was worried. PJ was always carefree, cracking jokes as easily as he breathed. Something must be really wrong.

"Look, I gotta put something in your mom's trunk. I'll get it out before morning, I swear to God, but I gotta put it in there right now." Patrick's stomach lurched. This sounded like trouble, but he knew he couldn't say no to his cousin.

"Dammit, PJ," he said, handing him the keys, "bring the keys right back and I swear if whatever it is isn't gone by 6:00 in the morning, I'm throwing it down the sewer."

PJ shot him a look of gratitude, snatched the keys and was gone without a word. Patrick said nothing when Slick came back to retrieve the jacket he'd forgotten. The fewer people who knew, the better.

Whatever was in the trunk haunted his thoughts as he and Kiley walked to the car, but by the time he was in the empty parking lot around the corner from his neighborhood, it was the farthest thing from his mind. The look in Kiley's eyes let him know his calculations had been correct, and soon they were in the back seat kissing and fumbling with each other's zippers and buttons.

Patrick had never been with a virgin before, and he was a little scared she would scream or change her mind. Twice he asked her if she wanted him to stop, and both times she told him to keep going. In the end she was quiet, but he felt her body tighten with pain and saw that her cheeks were stained with tears when he was done. He kissed her neck, and held her as long as he felt like he could before he had to drive her home.

CHAPTER 7

Suffolk County Jail, June 1991

"SO WHAT ARE you doing in here, young man?" the counselor asked. "I saw your record. No priors. Catholic school, even."

"I'm here because I was in the wrong place at the wrong time," Prospect said bluntly. "It's not that complicated."

"I hear you. I'm sure that had a lot to do with it," she admitted, trying to sound sympathetic. "But everyone in here also made certain decisions that led to getting arrested. No one ends up here by purely by accident."

"You sure about that?" he asked, raising his eyebrows quizzically.

"I see you have a tattoo," the counselor remarked, trying a different tactic to get him to open up. "Looks pretty new. What does it mean to you?"

He shrugged. "Not sure what it means now. It meant something when I got it."

"I'm not that familiar with the *Bible*," she said. "Can you tell me what verse that is?

His eyes remained fixed on the floor, he stayed silent for a long time. Finally he spoke, "It's about God and vengeance."

"And why did you choose that verse?" she asked.

"It's a long story."

"I've got plenty of time."

CHAPTER 8

November 1990

NATE SQUIRMED IN the pew next to his mother. The weather had already started turning cold, but he was sweating in his starched shirt and Sunday suit. It seemed unfair that he should have to dress up on Sunday, even though he had to wear a uniform all week. But he knew better than to press his case with Mom.

Sunday mornings were yet another fixture of Nate's life that remained almost completely predictable. The hymns the choir sang varied, as did the featured text in the *Bible* that Reverend Gibbs's sermon would explore. Today, it was Romans 12:9, "Dearly beloved, avenge not yourselves, but rather give place unto wrath: for it is written, Vengeance is mine; I will repay, saith the Lord." But the feel of the sanctuary, the sway of the choir and the cadence in Reverend Gibbs's preaching were always the same.

Nate glanced around without moving his head too much. The pews were nearly full. He estimated that about two thirds of the congregants were retirement age, while the rest were mostly mothers and their children. Two notable exceptions were the Andersons and the Gates: both men had their arms stretched around their wives' shoulders, while their children sat quietly next to them. Andre was sitting with his two younger brothers two rows in front. Aunt Carol was off to the left.

The collection plate was passed, and Nate's mother put in twenty dollars as she did every single week, no matter how tight things had been. Sometimes it made Nate wince; that was a dinner at a restaurant or something nice (on sale) for his mom's closet. But, as she told him over and over, she would never rob God. There were all sorts of ways the Lord sustained them that they couldn't always see, she reminded him. She still had her job, even when others had been fired or let go. And they had both been healthy, she pointed out. And think about how long things like the vacuum cleaner had lasted! Twenty years old almost, and still working like it was brand new. Same with her winter coat and her snow boots.

Nate wasn't so sure all that was connected to giving money to the church, but that never diminished his opinion of his mom. She was not one of those churchgoers who constantly expected God to rescue them from their own terrible decisions. She worked hard, spent little, and taught her boy to stay out of trouble. Why wouldn't God want to help a woman like that?

When service ended, they filed into the fellowship hall for dinner, since it was the first Sunday of the month. That was a ritual that Nate still relished, mostly because it was one of the few times where his mother's neuroticism about healthy eating was suspended, and he was allowed to pile his plate with whatever he wanted until he was completely satisfied.

And those church mothers could *cook*. Fried chicken, mac and cheese, smoked brisket, and tender ribs with meat falling off the bone, along with mashed potatoes and gravy, sweet potato casserole, corn pudding, green beans with bacon and collards with as much ham as leafy greens. Then there were baskets piled high with buttery biscuits and soft yeast rolls, and trays full of as many different kinds of cakes and pies as you could imagine.

Nate would eat a little of everything—encouraged by the mothers to take more—and then go back for seconds, until he felt like he couldn't move. In recent years, he had begun to understand that many of these elderly folks had grown up feeling hungry, and that nothing gave them as much pleasure as watching young people eating their fill with no concern for running out. And come to think of it, maybe giving that twenty every week helped his mom know she was contributing her fair share to these feasts—and the rest of the church's activities—even if people like the Andersons probably gave way more.

"You ready for basketball tryouts?" Andre asked, as Nate sat down at the long table across from him. Andre was a sophomore and another one of the hundred black kids who had gotten a scholarship to Cathedral High School.

"Yeah, it should go fine. I don't know too much about the team, but they're not bad for a small Catholic school, I've heard. You gonna play too?" Nate asked.

"My mom wants me to focus on school," Andre said with a sigh. "I got a C in math last quarter and she almost took my head off."

"Well, that sucks. They'll be a few scouts at the Cathedral games, but it's all about BNBL summer league, man. Are you gonna be able to do that?"

"Yeah, I think so. My uncle in North Carolina said he'd take care of the fees. His shop had a good year," Andre said. "What about you?"

"Yeah, we're good. My dad had a pension," Nate said. "It wasn't a lot, but Mom puts it all away for stuff like that." There were times Nate wondered what it was like for kids to live like they did on The Cosby Show or Family Ties, where money was never a problem and the biggest issue the family had to deal with was a hilarious misunderstanding. Oddly though, those shows didn't make him feel angry or resentful. They were more like a window into another world, a world he wanted to be part of one day.

Later that afternoon, Nate heard a banging on the apartment door. He checked the peephole and saw it was Slugs and his brother Tre. They were wearing black and grey sports jerseys and jeans. Aunt Carol had given up trying to force them to go to church a long time ago. Nate unbolted both locks and let them in.

"Where your mom at?" Tre asked, throwing himself on the couch.

"Still at church for a meeting. She'll be back in like an hour." The last sentence was a mild warning. Slugs and Tre were allowed in the apartment, because they were family. But if Mom got home she would definitely start interrogating them about their grades, their lack of church attendance and the high top fade Tre was trying to grow. She would also have insisted on addressing them by their given names, which they both hated.

"Yo, Nate, you heard about Ricky's plan?" Slugs asked anxiously. Ricky! That had been the huge man that Nate had bumped into on his way to the basketball court the first day of school, and he couldn't remember seeing him since. Ricky had been friends with Troy, and Nate knew that Aunt Carol sometimes wondered if Troy's death had been connected to his friendship with Ricky.

"I saw him like a couple months ago. What's he doing?" Nate asked, taking the bait. His cousins were always dreaming up new schemes to get rich or famous. Sometimes their ideas were harmless, like buying candy in bulk and selling it at school, which might have worked if Slugs hadn't eaten most of the inventory himself. Other times they were shadier, like prying hub caps off out-of-state cars and selling them to the local garage. Nate usually indulged their dreams by letting them talk without paying too much attention.

"Ricky just got back from Miami," Slugs explained. "He met a dude last time he was locked up who used to be muscle for Castle Gate, but the man don't run with them no more. The Castle boys thought he was a dumb sonofabitch, so they said all kind of shit in front of him. But actually, he's like really smart, and he's got cousins in Miami with a supplier connection to South America or whatever." Slugs waved his hand in the general direction where he imagined South America was. "The dude's bringing Ricky on and they looking for someone to distribute for them on our block and east of here. Me and Tre's gonna be in on the ground floor and rise real quick."

Nate's heart leaped in his chest, but he controlled his reaction. It would have been one thing if one or both of his cousins had announced they were going to push for Castle Gate like Rodney. Half the boys in their neighborhood would do that at some point in their lives, and probably half of those would end up dead or locked up. But starting a competitive gang was akin to a suicide pact. He looked at his cousins' Jerseys with the word "Kings" on them—which he had initially assumed was a homage to Motown or something—and remembered the new Norfolk Kings graffiti he had started noticing around town. How long had they been cooking up this scheme? How deep were they in?

He took a deep breath and looked at both of them in the eyes. "Listen to me," he said with a deadly intensity in his voice. "You are out of your goddamn minds if you come near this kind of shit. A new gang? Are you serious? You got Castle Gate on one side of you and you'll run into the Irish on Adams Corner and Savin Hill, never mind those crazy white dudes from Hecla Street. All of them will shoot down a couple black kids tryin to run up in their territory without blinking. How can you not understand that?"

"Maybe we shoot them first," Tre shot back defiantly. Nate's eyes lowered to a bulge under Tre's shirt and realized his cousin was already carrying. "You think I'm pissing my drawers over Castle

Gate or some goddamn Irish boys? Do they even move shit down there anyway? I thought they was all about the horse racing." Tre and Slugs laughed. The legendary Irish criminal network didn't strike fear into their hearts the way it did to the Irish enclaves of Boston. They were too young to remember all the missing bodies in the seventies and eighties, and their own streets held enough other dangers to keep them occupied.

"I have no idea," Nate answered, rolling his eyes. "I don't care what they do over there. Some say they run shit, others say their big man just collects tribute from the other dealers, including Castle Gate. I don't know and I don't care. But I am damn sure they won't put up with a coupla black kids selling shit in their territory. And if you can't see that, I don't know how the hell to help you." Nate's mother forbade him to use the N-word, no matter how much he wanted to sometimes. And this was definitely one of those times.

"I told Slugs you wouldn't be in," Tre said, shaking his head with a condescending disappointment. "That's cool. You got your books and your ball, and I don't hate you for it. But I thought I'd offer you the opportunity, since you family and all."

"Look," Nate said, deadly serious. "I'm begging you not to do this. Your mom's already worried—"

"You look," Tre returned, equally serious. "I'll always take care of my mom, and I will beat the living shit out of anyone who says I won't. But she don't know nothin about what it's like out there. She works all day at her shitty job and spends the rest of her time at church. She don't understand how the real world works. I know you're gonna go to college and make it big in the League or in business or being a doctor of whatever the hell you decide to do. How am I gonna get my mom outa Dorchester, huh? Working at the goddamn Kmart?"

"You can't look at it like that," Nate protested, knowing already it was a pointless argument. "You gotta look at where you are and think about your options—"

"Shut the hell up, Nate!" Tre said. "Don't give me all that shit about options. You have options. You even at school with all the white boys now. It's fine with me if you don't want to be in with what we're doin. But you sure as hell ain't gonna tell me what to do."

"Fine," Nate said, putting up his hands in surrender and shooting Slugs an angry glance. He didn't think Tre would actually pull his gun on him, but there was no point in continuing to argue. More than anything at that moment, he wished Troy was still alive. Troy had been calm, but funny, tough but sensible. He would have known exactly what to say to shut Tre up. "Fine. Have it your way."

"You ain't gonna tell Mom—" Slugs protested.

"Of course not," Nate rolled his eyes again. "I won't have to. Aunt Carol isn't stupid. She's going figure it out soon enough."

CHAPTER 9

THE AUTUMN SUN illuminated the spectacular stained glass windows that reached up for what seemed like miles. The smell of incense was almost overwhelming, but everyone knew the priests went heavy on it to help cover the smell of the homeless who often received ministry within the walls of the cathedral. Majestic atmosphere aside, 9:00 a.m. always felt early on a Sunday, and Patrick was dosing off between the prayers.

The enormous Gothic style limestone building dated back to 1875. It was one of the largest and most important cathedrals in the United States, and arguably the most beautiful. It was here, Patrick's mother reminded him, that the cardinal had celebrated a Requiem Mass for President Kennedy after his assassination. The Holy Father himself had visited in 1979. And although he sometimes felt ambivalent about waking up for it, Patrick was proud to go to Mass here.

He jolted back to consciousness when it was time to take communion. He filed forward with the rest of the people in his row, knelt at the altar as he had hundreds of times before, and received the bread from the priest. As he chewed and swallowed, he briefly imagined it as the actual flesh of Christ. The thought had always given him a strange thrill that he didn't fully understand.

As his family filed out, he caught a glimpse of Kiley, her little brothers and her parents walking down an aisle parallel to his own. She smiled at him but said nothing. They had only been able to repeat their dalliance once since homecoming, when Kiley faked a headache to get out of a visit to a relative's home. But the scarcity of their liaisons made them all the more desirable, and while sometimes Patrick didn't think about her at all, when he did, he thought he might be willing to die for her.

Back home, he shed his Sunday clothes the way he shed his uniform after school each day, leaving them on his floor. He pulled on his jeans, a t-shirt and a Celtics sweatshirt, put his Marky Mark and the Funky Bunch cassette in his Walkman, and lay down on his bed. He had some homework, but it was still early. His ma was headed to work, dropping his sisters off at a cousin's on the way, so he had the house to himself.

Patrick glanced briefly at the short stack of college applications on his desk; Father Lydon had reminded him that the first parts were due very soon. He had started his essays on a legal pad—Ma had never gotten around to buying a computer like he kept bugging her to—but most of what he wrote sounded stupid when he reread it. He had always done pretty well in English, although he preferred math. But somehow sitting down to write five paragraphs about yourself just seemed pointlessly annoying.

He was getting sleepy. For a second he imagined his dad was back, standing in the doorway. Would he be proud he was applying to school? Or would he laugh that he was wasting his time? The image faded quickly as he dozed off.

He woke to a banging on his front door. For a second he thought it might be Kiley, but the noise was way too loud. He ran downstairs and opened the door. It was PJ.

"Your ma gone?" he asked.

"Yeah, she dropped the girls at Aunt Aileen's before work."

"Perfect," PJ said, pulling out a six-pack and a bottle of cheap whiskey from under his jacket.

"I'm fine with a beer," Patrick said, eying the bottle with some surprise. He had never known his cousin to want anything heavier. "What'd you do? Raid the folks' liquor cabinet?"

"Nah, my dad keeps track of that shit," PJ laughed. "Sean swiped it from work. They go through so much there in a weekend, they won't notice if one bottle goes missing as long as it's not top shelf."

"Is Sean gonna learn to bartend?" Patrick asked "He's almost 21. They pull pretty good money there, I heard, especially on the weekends."

"Nah, he's got bigger plans," PJ said vaguely, laughing like it was funny somehow.

"Like what?"

"Entrepreneurship. Running with the big dogs. You know, shit like that." PJ grinned.

"You mean joining up with Franky Riley and his crew?" Patrick asked.

PJ shrugged his shoulders noncommittally. After his sudden disappearance in 1980, some had mumbled that Patrick's dad had been killed by one of Whitey's lieutenants over a poker game that ended up with Patrick's Dad knocking out three wise guys. Others insisted he had another family in Ireland, or even that he had run off to join Sinn Fein. If Ma knew, she kept it to herself. For whatever reason, Patrick rarely asked about any of it.

But he had asked lots of questions about Irish organized crime: what they did, how much money they made, and why no matter who got arrested, Whitey always seemed untouchable. Ma's answers were always brief and unsatisfying. The Winter Hill Gang had excited

Patrick's imagination since he was a child, as they had probably every other boy in his neighborhood.

Patrick's fascination cut both ways. On the one hand, he knew good and well that you shouldn't join up with a bunch of loan sharks and bookies when you could go to college and make something more of yourself. And, if he was honest, he knew plenty of people Whitey had terrorized over the years, whether or not he'd actually done his old man in. On the other hand, just as many saw him as a protector. Patrick's aunt—one of the prettiest girls at Southie in her youth— would get endlessly catcalled on her walk home from school during the late 1960s. One word from Whitey to the harassers, however, and she had never been bothered again. Love him or hate him, everyone knew it was Whitey's world. If you were breathing, it was because he was letting you live in it.

Patrick knew his neighborhood well, he always listened and took notice of the wise guys and the who's who in the organized crews, or whose dad was "really connected". Recently he would run into

Whitey often, because ever since Whitey had won the lottery, Nana wanted him to buy her lottery tickets down at the Rotary. She would say "Somehow that bastard has a horseshoe of Irish luck up his ass, we need our lottery tickets and our scratchies from there ever week!" Patrick enjoyed running his weekly errand as he knew most of the guys that worked down at the Rotary and the South Boston Liquor Mart, when he crossed paths with Whitey, Whitey would always give him a respectable head nod. He wondered if the gesture was in any way related to the rumors of his dad.

Patrick laughed at the thought of Sean rising through their ranks as he opened a can of beer and switched on the TV. Football was on, and the Patriots were busy racking up one their fifteen losses in what would be a franchise-worst season.

"What the hell is wrong with them?" PJ asked in disgust as the quarterback was sacked for a 12-yard loss. "It's like they're not even trying."

"Jesus, PJ," Patrick said, noticing how much of the whiskey PJ was drinking. "There's school tomorrow."

"Yeah, maybe," he replied, lighting a cigarette. "Maybe there's not for me."

"Look, I know it's just Southie, but you really shouldn't skip all the time," Patrick said. He was trying not to sound too much like a parent, but he was starting to really worry about his cousin, who had seemed less and less like himself as the weeks went by.

"What's the big deal?" PJ asked, genuinely confused. "I'll probably pass everything. It's not like I'm going to college like you, anyway, so what's the point?"

"That's not what I mean," Patrick said. "Just cause you don't wanna go to college doesn't mean school doesn't matter. Do you even know what you wanna do?"

PJ took another swig from the bottle, shrugged his shoulders, and teased gently, "No, Ma, I don't know what I wanna do. Don't worry, Paddy. I'll figure something out."

Patrick dropped the subject. Senior year wasn't turning out quite the way he had expected anyway. He liked being at the top of the food chain at school, of course. But the path in front of him looked increasingly uncertain. He knew he'd get his college applications done eventually, and that he'd be going somewhere next year. But the more he thought about it, the more he realized he had no idea what he should study, or what college would even be like. He had never stepped foot on a campus and hadn't really known anyone who had gone away and graduated.

Some of his older high school friends were now away at various schools, of course. They came home in the summer with tales of frat parties, sorority girls, and football games. They all seemed to be doing fine, and he assumed he would do fine too. But the whole thing was an unknown quantity. In some ways he couldn't wait for high school to be over, but in other ways he wished that it could last forever. Being popular and told you have potential was one thing. Going out and proving it was another matter altogether.

"Hey, didn't your old man have a gun?" PJ asked out of the blue, as the game broke for half time.

"Yeah, why?" Patrick asked. Guns were all over the Boston neighborhoods, of course. But he had never known PJ to need one.

"You still have it around?" he persisted, ignoring the question.

"No, it disappeared when he did. What the hell do you need a gun for?" Patrick pressed. "Listen. If there is a beef at school and the n*ggers want to drive by the park or the corner and light us up, we're screwed!" PJ exclaimed.

"It's not for me anyways," PJ insisted. "It's for someone else. No worries. I will just get it from Kevin down D Street."

" Sure it is, Patrick thought to himself."

CHAPTER 10

THE CONFLICT WITH his cousins had put Nate in a bad mood for several reasons. First, he was now in a very awkward position if his mother interrogated him again over Slugs and Tre's behavior. He would cover for them, of course. Just because you were a good kid didn't mean you had to snitch. But Mom was incredibly skilled at sniffing out lies, omissions and half-truths. She was also fully capable of making his life miserable if she sensed he was holding back information.

Second, he felt worried for his cousins, especially Slugs, who was slower to think things through and seemed increasingly willing to go along with whatever Tre said or did since Troy had died. Whatever carefree optimism they once had seemed to have been lowered into the ground with their big brother. To them, life was a battle to stay alive, and eventually everyone was going to lose.

Nate knew Tre would look out for himself, and he would tell himself he was looking out for his younger brother. But Nate could easily imagine Slugs getting in over his head fast. Part of him wanted to get Slugs alone and try to talk sense into him, but then he knew Tre's constant presence would be too strong an influence to overcome with one conversation.

Still, Nate told himself, most likely the scheme would come to nothing, like all their other ideas. Maybe the supplier angle that Ricky was bragging about wasn't real, or it wouldn't pan out. Then they'd have to forget about the whole thing. Would they even be able to figure out the technical side of things? Where would they cook and store everything without getting raided by the police? Surely they wouldn't be stupid enough to try to bring any product into Aunt Carol's house.

Then there was the level of nerve it took. Nate's friend Rodney was a cool customer; always had been. Would Slugs really be able to hand off a vial smoothly without attracting attention? Would he be able to spot the difference between an undercover cop and a real customer, or demonstrate all those other intangible skills that determined who survived and who got locked up? Nate's doubts haunted him all day at school until the bell rang and it was time to change for basketball tryouts.

———

Patrick had finished lifting weights with the strength coach after school in preparation for hockey tryouts. There was no question he would be team captain again this year, but he didn't want to leave any room for doubt. On his way to the locker room to shower, he heard the noises of basketball tryouts and paused in the doorway to see if he could catch Slick.

Slick stood there with about 40 other boys, probably ten of them black. All of them looked sweaty.

"Okay, I want guards to my right, forwards to my left and any big men who want to play center, just stay where you are and I'll come to you," Coach Kelly commanded.

Patrick watched Slick and Nate move over to the section with the guards—joining about eight other boys—to await instructions.

Coach Kelly came over and told them to begin dribbling with their right hands, clicking his stopwatch to mark their time. He watched each boy closely, and the told them to immediately switch to their left hands. Nate looked focused but relaxed, like he'd done this hundreds of times before. Patrick noticed many of the others beginning to lose control as the seconds ticked by.

Next came free throws, which Patrick imagined must have been more difficult than normal after all that dribbling. Coach Kelly watched them all shoot, marking how many went in. Patrick saw only one of Nate's shots miss, while four of Slick's were short or rimmed out. Finally, they were allowed a water break, sending the boys into the hall for the water fountain.

"Hey, when are you done?" Patrick asked Slick as the boys all took turns getting drinks. He noticed all the black students, including Nate, walked to the water fountain further down the hall by the old visitors' locker room.

"At least another hour," Slick said, rolling his eyes. "You should just go. I'll catch up with you later."

"How's it going in there?" Patrick asked, not indicating he had watched.

"Well, the good news is, we'll probably win a few more games this year. The bad news is, I might be coming off the bench." Slick seemed irritated but resigned to his fate.

"But you're a senior," Patrick protested.

"Yeah, and all those kids are juniors or younger," Slick agreed, shaking his head. "It'll be one thing if that shitty kid who took my locker starts ahead of me, because he's pretty damn good. But the rest of them might be getting a bullshit Affirmative Action spot..." Slick's voice trailed off.

Patrick nodded and watched Slick walk back into the gym. The black kids were walking back too, when someone on the PA system called Coach Kelly to the office for a phone call. All the boys seemed visibly relieved to have an extra few minutes to rest. At the end of the day, sweat had no color, Patrick thought.

"Do you play year-round?" Patrick asked Nate.

"Nah," Nate answered like it was no big deal. "BNBL summer league, though."

"No shit. That's cool. I play hockey and I box in the summer," Patrick explained.

"That's cool. I always liked watching boxing, but my mom would kill me if I even thought about taking it up," Nate laughed. "They don't have that in college, do they?"

"I don't think so," Patrick said. "You trying to play ball in college?"

"We'll see," Nate said. "No guarantee, but never say never."

"You'll probably get recruited," Patrick encouraged him. "I've never seen anyone from our school handle Coach Kelly's drills that easy."

"Thanks, but there's hundreds more kids in the country who dribble just as well as me or way better," Nate explained. "I got a shot, but I'm not a sure thing. My older cousin was being recruited by a few schools until he caught a goddamn stray, just walking down the street to buy a Coke from the corner store."

"He die?" Patrick asked.

"Yup. After ten days in the hospital. Woke up long enough to say bye to my Aunt Carol."

Patrick wasn't sure what to say, so he said, "Shit."

"Makes you wonder what the point is," Nate sighed, almost to himself. "Troy kept his head down, did his homework, didn't bang, didn't smoke reefer, didn't piss off Castle Gate, but he caught a bullet just the same." The two stood there by the water fountain for a second without saying anything. The rest of the boys had returned to the gym. "But anyway," Nate said, switching back to normal conversation, "Summer League is where the recruiters come to watch.

Not too many gonna make the trip to the Catholic Conference League just to see us here."

"Yeah, I guess that's right. But you're really good. You should keep following your dream, and all that shit," Patrick encouraged him.

Nate laughed. "Thanks, man. So what's *your* dream then? What're you doing here, wearing a uniform and doing homework when you could be sleeping through class at Southie and making straight A's?"

Patrick paused. Why was it so hard to answer such an easy question? "I dunno. But maybe start a business or go into politics. Maybe follow the Kennedy path! How about you? The Michael Jordan or the Martin Luther King route?"

"You're not suggesting we follow the path that gets us both shot in the head, are you?" Nate asked. He raised his eyebrows and laughed. "Okay. So you're gonna go to Hahvahd, then?" he queried, pronouncing it with an exaggerated Kennedy-esque accent.

"Yeah right," Patrick laughed. "Maybe BC or BU. I dunno. I'll figure it out."

"Well, where are you even applying?" Nate asked seriously. "Regular application deadlines are in January. Early decision already passed. You know that, right?"

"Of course!" Patrick shot back defensively. But in reality he had been avoiding the stack of applications on his desk. "I'll go where I get in. No big deal."

"What's your safety?" Nate asked.

Before Patrick could answer, the coach called everyone back to divide into teams to play five-on-five and demonstrate their knowledge of running pick-and-rolls and screens, as well three-two and two-three defenses. Patrick was irritated now, and had no more interest in watching Nate dominate the others.

Back at home, Patrick's feelings of annoyance gave way to a burning anxiety over his college applications. His mother, however, was up in arms over the idea that Slick might lose the starting point guard job to an upstart junior from Dorchester.

"What the hell, Paddy?" she ranted. "They can't do that to him! His parents paid for him to go to that school for four goddamn years. And some little n*gger from Dorchester thinks he can just take his spot? That's reverse racism for you."

"Jesus Christ, Ma," Patrick groaned, "Do you not watch television? Robert Parish, Reggie Lewis, Magic Johnson, Michael Jordan? Lots of black people are good at basketball. It's like a known fact."

"I don't give a damn!" his mother shot back. "He's a senior. It's his spot."

"Ma, it's not a big deal. Slick doesn't even care. Besides Nate plays in BNBL summer league. That's a big deal." He felt a touch of resentment as he uttered the last sentence. It wasn't like he nurtured big dreams of boxing professionally or playing in the NHL, but it did occur to him that he'd never really given it his best shot. What could he have done in the hockey rink if he'd really focused and given his all? He'd never know.

He thought again about Nate's performance in tryouts. Nate hadn't just looked fast and strong. He'd looked intensely, expertly prepared. It was that preparation—that sense that he knew exactly what the world would demand of him and how to deliver it—that was beginning to make Patrick feel less sure of himself.

"Ma, what do people mean when they talk about applying to a 'safety'? Like for college."

She pulled out a cigarette from her purse, lit it and answered, "Damned if I know, Paddy. Ask the goddamned counselor at school, if she's not too busy helping all the n*ggers. That's why we pay all that money for you to go there."

CHAPTER 11

THERE WERE ONLY a couple of hockey practices over Christmas break, but Patrick had decided to work out in the weight room on a free morning, despite how tired he felt. The holidays meant greater freedom, and he, Walsh and PJ had stayed up pretty late the night before drinking beers. Sean had shown up well past midnight on a brand new motorcycle, which probably meant he really was doing something criminal after all. There was no way he could've afforded something like that on a busboy salary.

Patrick swallowed some Advil, put on his coat, and rode his bike to the school through the freezing cold. The wind bit his face as he kept his head down to try to minimize his exposure. Just because you were used to winter didn't mean you enjoyed it.

Boston was his home, and Patrick knew every last brick and graffiti mark in Southie. Still, sometimes he had to pause and consider how crazy his town must have looked to outsiders. World-renown academic institutions stood just blocks from some of the worst crime and poverty in the country. Each little neighborhood was like a separate world, with its own unique wonders and perils.

South Boston IRA Mural

Patrick locked up his bike and tried the front door of the school. It was locked, but Father Lydon emerged from his office and opened it, smiling warmly at him.

"Here to use the weight room?" he asked.

"You know it," Patrick answered, smiling despite his headache.

"You'll have it almost all to yourself," Father Lydon laughed. Patrick was a little surprised. Hardly anyone else on the hockey team did extra weight training, and certainly not over winter break. As he pushed open the door to the weight room, he saw Nate, working on his traps on the universal weights.

"Oh hey," Patrick said, slightly annoyed for reasons he couldn't quite identify. He had started the school year intrigued and some-what fascinated by his new classmate. Now he was starting to feel like maybe he had had enough.

"Hey," Nate nodded to him, continuing with his set.

"You mind spotting me?" Patrick asked as he removed his sweat-shirt. Might as well take advantage of the company.

"Sure," Nate said amiably. "Just a second." Nate finished his reps, wiped the sweat off his face and hands, and walked over to the bench press.

"You mail in those applications?" Nate asked, as Patrick began his first set. He tone was friendly.

Shit, thought Patrick. He really was almost done with them, but the disruption in routine around the holidays had put them far from his mind. And he was in no mood for friendly reminders.

"What the hell would you know about that?" Patrick demanded, as he forced the barbell up. "You're just a junior."

"Never mind then," Nate said, brushing off the insult and helping Patrick get the bar back into its cradle. He spotted Patrick for two more sets in silence. He then began doing curls with hand weights, watching his form in the mirror. Patrick worked on the leg press, loading probably more weight than he needed. He thought he saw Nate raise his eyebrows, but he couldn't be sure.

"Well, I'm done. You need another spot before I go?" Nate asked.

"Nah, I'm good," Patrick said, not wanting Nate's help with anything anymore.

"Okay, see ya," Nate said, putting on his sweats and coat and heading for the door. He opened it and paused, "Listen. Applications are due really soon. You should really make sure you get them in the mail."

"Why the hell do you always have to act like you know everything?" Patrick demanded. Even as he heard the words come out of his mouth, he knew they sounded petty.

"What the hell are you talking about?" Nate asked, his eyes narrowing; Patrick saw the sudden return of the hardened demeanor that he had seen the first day of school when Slick had tried to block Nate's locker.

"Who the hell are you to talk to me about college applications?" Patrick asked, unable to back down. "What do you know about any of it? *Your* parents go to college or something?"

Nate dropped his bag, and took two steps toward Patrick, letting the door close behind him. "Oh, so I live in the shitty part of Dorchester, and you think because I don't talk ghetto all the time or smoke reefer that I'm rising above my place?" Nate asked. "Is the nigga getting too high-minded fo ya, Massa?" He uttered the forbidden word with an exaggerated Southern drawl.

"Shut up!" Patrick shot back, his cheeks flushed with rage. "How the hell are you gonna talk to me like that? Do you even know how much I stick up for you? I've never said that word to you or about you. Ever."

"Am I supposed to thank you for that?" Nate asked with a smirk. "Am I supposed to tell you that you're one of the 'good white people' who wouldn't have owned slaves or lynched anyone if you had lived back in the day?"

"What the hell, man?" Patrick retorted, realizing Nate could dish it out just as well as he could take it. "You think the Irish had it any easier? We were treated like shit just like you and your people, remember the Irish were the n-word of the white race!" "No one would hire us..." Patrick stopped himself. He sounded just like his mother. Even more infuriating, Nate was chuckling in disbelief.

"Look, Patrick, Paddy, whatever the hell you want me to call you." Nate said, as he wiped the tears of laughter from his face. "It's not a contest. I'm sure you Irish have your problems, and I'm playing the world's tiniest violin for ya. But lemme ask you this: have I *ever* bitched to you about how hard it is to be black?"

Patrick said nothing.

"Exactly," Nate returned triumphantly. "And I never will, because I don't need your goddamn pity. And whatever you may think, I'm not trying to show off. I know who I am, and I know where I come from. I keep my nose clean, because I don't have the luxury of getting wasted and stoned every day and then pulling my shit together when I feel like growing up. I screw up once, I'm in jail for life or dead. That's the way that it is for someone like me, whether you see it or not. And I'm not saying that so you'll feel sorry for me. I'm just telling you how it is."

"Well, it's not like my life has been perfect either," Patrick protested. He almost brought up his dad's disappearance, but thought better of it. "But I don't as hell don't need *your* help to make something of it."

"Whatever," Nate said, rolling his eyes and picking up his bag. "I know you think I can't possibly know what I'm talking about, because how could a little black boy know something that you don't know? Well let me tell you: my mom may be stuck cleaning hotel rooms for shit money, but if that woman wants to find something out, she will talk to every living soul on God's green earth until someone tells her. Before I even enrolled here, she took a half-day off from work and came to the school. She met with the counselors and wrote down everything they told her I needed to do to get into college. She repeated everything on that list to me every single goddamn day since then. And from what they told her, it's good to apply to at least one safety school and finish your goddamn applications before New Year's. I know that's what I'll do next year. But if telling you that makes you feel bad, then I'll just keep my damn mouth shut."

"Sounds great to me," Patrick said, as Nate rolled his eyes and walked out, letting the door slam behind him. Patrick did a few more sets on the universal and found that he still felt like crap; the Advil had worn off, his head throbbed and he was almost dehydrated enough to puke. He privately resolved not to stay up late tonight, started putting his sweats back on preparation to leave. As he headed back to the lobby, he noticed the light was still on in Father Lydon's office. He paused at the water fountain and took a drink.

He knew the argument with Nate was stupid before it even

started, and he already felt a little embarrassed about how he had behaved. Even though part of him would have liked to fight, just to discharge his emotions, he was glad it hadn't ended up coming to blows. Still, he was starting to get a grip on how his feelings toward Nate had changed. For the first time it dawned on him: Nate actually felt sorry for *him*. An underprivileged junior from the bad part of Dorchester who had to come here on a full scholarship because his mom barely made minimum wage could easily see that he— Patrick, the pride of his family—didn't have a damn clue what he was going to do with his future and was trying to offer him advice. It was too humiliating to even contemplate.

He drank some more water and wiped the sweat off his forehead with his towel. Calmer now, Patrick knocked on Father Lydon's door and entered as the kind voice inside told him to.

"So I just had a quick question for you, Father" Patrick said. He didn't sit down, since he didn't plan to stay long.

"Of course," Father Lydon said warmly, looking up from his papers.

"What do people mean when they talk about applying to a 'safety school'?" he asked.

"Patrick," Father Lydon said, concern evident in his voice. "Haven't you met with your counselor about your college applications? They're due in just a couple of weeks."

"Oh, I filled out all the personal information, and I'm almost done with most of the essays," Patrick said, trying to downplay the fact that he hadn't mailed them yet. "What else is there?"

"You have to secure teacher and counselor recommendations, and you have to submit your test scores to each school..."

"Oh..."Patrick stumbled. He hadn't really read the instructions on the front of the applications all that carefully. "Well, is it too late?"

"No, no," Father Lydon said, eager to reassure him. "I'll help you take care of it. Hang on." The priest got up from behind his desk and rushed across the hall, returning with a folder. Patrick took a seat. Like everything else in his life these days, this was turning out to be way more complicated than he thought it was going to be.

"This is your file," Father Lydon explained, as he skimmed the papers inside. "Let's see here. Okay, I see your SAT's aren't bad, just above the national average. Now, where are you applying?"

"So far, Northeastern, BU and BC," Patrick said. "I don't want to go too far from home."

Father Lydon raised his eyebrows, not too differently from how Nate had done when Patrick had named those schools to him over a month ago. "Okay, those are fine schools, Patrick. Fine goals for a young man like you. But they might be called 'reach' schools for you, which means that you are not guaranteed to gain admission, and you'll likely need financial aid to attend. To your question, a 'safety' school is one where you are highly likely to be admitted."

"Why am I not 'likely' to get admitted to BU or BC?" Patrick asked, hurt and offended. Father Lydon had always encouraged him and believed in him; why this sudden change?

"Well, son, BU, BC and Northeastern may not be Harvard, but they are some of the top colleges in the country. Your grades aren't bad and your test scores are nothing to be ashamed of, but you understand that there are kids all over the country who have straight A's and get nearly a perfect score on the SAT, and lots of them apply to schools like that." Father Lydon's voice was kind, but had a tone of caution. It reminded him of Nate talking about all the talented kids in the country when discussing his own prospects for a basketball scholarship.

"But President Kennedy came from—" Patrick began.

"Yes," Father Lydon interrupted gently. "Yes, President Kennedy went to Harvard, and from what I have heard his test scores weren't actually all that impressive. But his father was already an extremely rich and powerful man, and fair or not, that kind of thing makes a big difference."

"So you think I shouldn't apply to those schools?"

"Of course you should apply," Father Lydon said. "There's absolutely nothing wrong with trying to go to any of those schools. I just think you should apply to some schools that are a little more realistic too."

"Like where?"

"Like Emerson, Suffolk and UMass Amherst. All those places would be good choices, and I can almost guarantee you'd be admitted to all three."

"Well, I don't have time to write more essays," Patrick said hesitantly. That wasn't exactly true. He had time; he just really, really didn't want to spend it that way.

"Of course," Father Lydon said sympathetically. "But most of the time, you can just edit the essays you've already written to fit the new questions. You never took that typing course I told you to take, did you?"

"I don't want to be a secretary," Patrick laughed.

"Sure," Father Lydon agreed with a patient smile. "But the future is computers, Paddy. I promise you, there will come a day soon when we won't handwrite notes and teachers won't write on the board anymore. Everything will be done on computers. Maybe there will be computers at every desk in classrooms someday, who knows?"

"Yeah, I'll learn to type someday," Patrick promised. "And I'll pick a safety school too."

"UMass Amherst has a later deadline," Father Lydon offered. "You'll find out later, of course, but I don't think you need to have everything postmarked until March 15."

"Thanks," Patrick said. The two exchanged a few more pleasantries and then said goodbye. Patrick always felt better after speaking to Father Lydon. He pulled the hood of his jacket over his face and walked out in the freezing cold to grab his bike. The sun had risen pretty high, but you could barely tell. The sky was gray and the air smelled like it might snow. He kept his head down slightly to prevent the wind from clawing at his cheeks and biked as quickly as he could, watching only the road in front of him.

Suddenly, his bike collided with someone running toward him. He almost fell as he put his foot down and felt two hands grab him by the shoulders. Instinctively, his body tensed up to fight.

"Paddy!" the voice shouted in his ear against the bitter wind.

"Walsh!" he answered, recognizing his friend.

"You've got to hurry. PJ's been shot!"

CHAPTER 12

THE VIGIL LAST night was a complete blur. Patrick didn't get completely wasted very often, but he had felt totally justified finishing a six-pack on his own at Sean's house, and chasing it with a few shots of whiskey. So had Walsh and a few of his other neighborhood friends who had walked over after church. Ma hadn't even tried to stop him.

What he still remembered vividly was rushing to the hospital and seeing PJ full of tubes with a respirator mask over his face just four short days before. He remembered cursing at whoever tried to keep him from rushing to the bedside. And he remembered all the machines beeping, the doctors rushing in and a nurse shoving him out of the room.

The whole incident was stamped on his brain like a traumatizing scene from a horror movie. The harder he tried not to think about it, the more clearly it played over and over in his head. His cousin, whom he'd known his entire life, was dead at 17, having bled out from two gunshot wounds to the leg. And Patrick felt paralyzed with grief and rage.

His head throbbed as the pipe organ played the first hymn at an unbearable volume. He could hear sobs at various places around the sanctuary. The priest's voice was solemn and steady, but Patrick failed to find comfort in it.

None of it made sense. PJ had apparently been shot in front of an apartment building on Ashmont, well to the west of Adams Street close to Dot Ave, which divided the Irish part of Dorchester from the black neighborhoods. No white kids walked in that area unless it was broad daylight and they were at least four deep. Even so, the trip would have to be absolutely necessary to be worth the risk. What the hell had PJ been doing there around midnight? Patrick's cousin had become a little reckless, sure, but he didn't have a death wish.

As the prayers continued, Patrick pondered what could possibly have possessed PJ. Had he been kidnapped? That didn't make sense. Trying to buy drugs? That was more believable, but still didn't ring true. PJ had begun to drink more liquor and smoke more weed than was good for him, but Patrick had never known him to experiment with anything like crack or heroin. What other reason was there to wander to the other side of Adams and Dot Ave? Could PJ have been killed somewhere else and then his body dumped where it was found? That seemed plausible, if a little farfetched.

Patrick glanced up and surveyed the pews. Everyone in the neighborhood was here, including distant cousins and friends from elementary school whom he hadn't seen in a while. It wasn't even noon, but Patrick began to think about when he could go back to bed. The service felt like it had been going on for hours. He knew he was supposed to remember his cousin and say goodbye, but right now he wanted more than anything to be somewhere else. Somewhere where PJ's death wasn't a reality anymore.

Finally, the Mass ended and people began to file out into the freezing cold street. They would drive to the cemetery in a procession with their lights on and a police escort. Then PJ's body would be lowered into the ground forever. Patrick would never see his cousin again.

As he neared the cathedral doors, Patrick recognized Sergeant Mike Daly, a city cop around his early fifties who had known Patrick's dad pretty well. They had run a Police Athletic League boxing club together down the "Muni" underneath the courthouse to keep kids off the street. He offered Patrick a sympathetic handshake.

Patrick always held his favorite picture of him and his father closely
in his nightstand drawer. Peter Welch's boxing gym.

"I'm real sorry about your cousin, Paddy. He was a good kid. It's a damn shame we lost him so young."

Patrick nodded, struggling to respond. He didn't want to cry, although he knew no one would blame him if he did. "They gonna catch the assholes who did it?" he asked, fighting to remain as stoic as possible.

"Well, son, I'm not assigned to the case," Sergeant Daly explained. "I heard some stuff around the station of course, and I'm really not supposed to share anything I know. But between us, it's going to be hard to figure out who did this. We're used to dealing with murders with a straightforward motivation. Money, gang affiliations, drugs, even stupid personal vendettas. But nobody seems to know why anyone would want to kill PJ."

Patrick nodded again, and said. nothing. He thought about the time PJ had asked him about his dad's old gun and wondered if he should mention it to Sergeant Daly.

"Look, PJ was found in a really bad part of town, and from what I heard they think he was there when he was shot. His body wasn't moved or anything. But of course they haven't been able to get any witnesses to come forward."

"Damn," Patrick said, mostly to himself.

"Can you think of any possible reason that PJ would go into that part of Dorchester by himself? He wasn't running with the wrong crew, was he?"

"No, no. Definitely not." PJ hadn't been himself lately, but it's not like he had started hanging out with a different crowd.

"Alright, well if you think of anything that might help the detectives, go down to the station and make a statement. They may be contacting you anyway. I'm sure they'll interview all his close friends and associates." Sergeant Daly said goodbye and Patrick went outside into the harsh sunlight to try to find his mother.

After the internment, Sean, Walsh and Patrick congregated at Walsh's house in the basement, taking turns playing each other in Streetfighter on his Nintendo.

"Look, the whole goddamn city is going to hell," Sean said, ruefully. The boys mumbled their agreement, but no one said much more.

"I'll tell you what, it's a goddamn shame that there are parts of Boston where a kid like PJ can't walk by himself. It didn't used to be like that. We used to own this whole city," Sean continued.

Walsh raised his beer. "You got that right!"

Even through the haze of grief and anger, Patrick knew that mythical version of Boston had started disappearing before they were born. They were losing Dorchester. Would they lose Southie someday too?

"We gotta do something about this, Paddy," Walsh said, trembling. "It's one thing to have n*ggers in our schools. They can shoot each other but its another if they think they can just shoot one of ours and nothing happens! They think we're softer than our parents' generation. They think we won't do a damn thing about it. We need to change that!"

"Now you're talking," Sean agreed.

"Look we don't even know who did it," Patrick said, exhausted. Part of him agreed with Walsh. But he couldn't help but think of what Father Lydon would say. He would say it was unfair to assume black people had killed PJ. And even if it turned out they had, Father Lydon would ask why they were getting more upset about that than they did when the Irish gangsters caused someone to "disappear."

"What do you mean we don't know?" Walsh protested. "Who the hell do you think was walking around Ashmont Street in the goddamn middle of the night?" True enough. Still, they had absolutely no hard evidence, and his conversation with Sergeant Daly made him doubtful that the cops were getting anywhere either.

"So what do you suggest we do?" Patrick asked. "Kill every black person we see? Or maybe we should go investigate on our own? Start wandering around the streets and asking questions?"

"You're right," Walsh agreed. "Before we do anything, we gotta figure out who did this."

"Don't worry," Patrick said. "I know just who to ask."

CHAPTER 13

Suffolk County Jail, July 1991

"YOU LOOK UPSET," the counselor observed.

"Wouldn't you be upset in my shoes?" Prospect asked.

"I suppose I would," she admitted. "But you look more upset than normal. What have you been thinking about?"

He said nothing and refused to meet her gaze.

"Have you been thinking about your mother, maybe? The detective in charge of the case said she works awfully hard to support you."

His bottom lip began to quiver, but he bit it to make it stop. "Shut up."

"Okay," she said gently. She had calculated that this line of inquiry might strike a nerve, but she was running out of ideas. He was so young, and he was facing a significant sentence for what her gut told her was no good reason. If she could just persuade him to tell the detectives what he knew about what had really happened that night, she felt confident his attorney would be able to get him out.

"From what I hear, you were the one everyone had really high hopes for. How do you think your mother feels, thinking about you locked up—"

"I said, SHUT UP!" He picked up the chair he was sitting in and flung it across the room, narrowly missing the counselor's head. Within seconds, the guards had come and restrained him, and he knew he would go back to solitary.

CHAPTER 14

"**I**'M REALLY SORRY about your cousin, man." Nate sounded unguarded and sincere, the characteristic edge gone from his voice. It was the first school day since Christmas break, and the two were at their lockers before school. Clearly, the tragedy was more than enough to cause him to overlook Patrick's behavior in the weight room.

"Thanks," Patrick said dully. Last Friday, Nate had scored 24 points and grabbed nine rebounds in Cathedral's win. Patrick's hockey game on the other hand, had been lackluster by his standards—one assist in a 2-2 tie—but he didn't care. He didn't care about anything except justice for PJ.

"Hey, you know I've been there. It sucks. It still hurts to think about Troy being gone. I know there's nothing I can do, but..." Nate's voice trailed off.

"Actually, there is," Patrick said, looking up at him.

"Hey, just name it," Nate said, reaching out and putting his hand on Patrick's shoulder.

"I need you to find out who did this," Patrick said, his voice deadly serious.

"Um, how the hell would I do that?" Nate asked with surprise, dropping his hand to his side and taking a step back. "I didn't even know your cousin."

"You live near Ashmont, don't you?"

"Yeah, but you know I don't bang," Nate reminded him.

"But you live there. You know everyone. Who runs those streets?"

"Castle Gate," Nate answered reflexively. "I do know a couple guys who push for them. I can ask around. But listen, I really don't know if I can find anything out."

"Just try," Patrick insisted.

"I will," Nate promised. "But listen, those guys are dangerous. They are stone cold killers, no question. But I really don't think they would kill a white boy over nothing, even in our part of town. No sane person wants to start turf war with the Irish Crews or Whitey wannabes."

It sounded strange to Patrick to hear that name come out of Nate's mouth. He remembered the mysterious package PJ stored in his trunk at homecoming and thought about his questions about the gun again. He had sensed for a while that his cousin was in over his head with something, but he never imagined that it would get him killed. "Yeah, PJ didn't run with those boys. He wasn't pure as the driven snow or anything, but he wasn't a gangsta, and he wasn't trying to be one."

"What the hell was he doing on Ashmont?" Nate asked.

"Damned if I know."

"Okay, listen. I'll find out what I can," Nate said, suddenly nervous about what he was getting himself into. "But I really can't promise anything. Some of those dudes won't think twice about capping someone like me if they think I'm trying to snitch. And if the cops pick that day to make a bust and I'm there, you think they're gonna believe I'm not just another gang-banger like the rest?"

"Look, I appreciate it, okay?" Patrick said. On the one hand, he knew enough by now to know that he was basically asking his friend to put his life on the line for him. He understood—as well as any outsider could—that Nate's life was a precarious balancing act, walking the straight and narrow path, while trying not to piss off or get tangled up with the jokers all around him. On the other hand, Patrick didn't care. Nothing mattered more than finding out what happened to PJ and why.

Nothing.

———

Weeks passed, though, and Nate wasn't able to find out very much. A conversation with Rodney yielded very little information. Rodney had heard about a white boy being popped in the black part of Dorchester, of course, but hadn't known who PJ was, what he was doing there, and insisted that Castle Gate had nothing to do with it. That was the standard response Nate would have expected, but Rodney had seemed sincere. That suggested to Nate that the slaying potentially came from higher up, and that someone on Rodney's level wouldn't be privy to the details.

Nate had mentioned it to Tre too. Tre and Slug's scheme to push for Ricky was moving along slowly, but relatively smoothly, to Nate's surprise. No one really knew who the Norfolk Kings were, or what they did, but they had been able to pick up a little trade in a three-block territory in a northern section of Dorchester that Castle Gate didn't patrol too closely. From time to time, Nate had noticed those telltale rolls of twenties in Tre's pocket that screamed "drug dealer." But other than that, he and Slugs seemed to be doing okay. Maybe, Nate thought, if they managed to stay in that small radius no man's land between their neighborhood and all the other gang territories they'd survive.

"Yo, why you care about that little punk ass white boy anyway?" Tre had demanded when Nate inquired. "You on their side now that you a Cathedral boy?"

"Are you serious, Tre?" Nate had responded in disgust. "He was my friend's cousin. He asked me if I knew anything about it. Just like I would've asked him if Troy been killed in Southie. Do you really not get that?"

"But Troy wasn't killed in Southie because he wasn't a stupid sonofabitch to wander over there. Can't say the same for your friend's cousin."

"Jesus, sorry I asked," Nate said. He hadn't expected such a strong reaction out of Tre, but those few rolls of twenties had caused his cousin to become pretty full of himself.

"Any goddamn fool knows that it takes the cops an hour to show up here," Tre laughed. "Why you think they never found Troy's killer? I knew from the time I heard that shot, won't nobody gonna find the man that shot my brother. Sounds like your white friend's about to find out how that feels."

Nate had to admit that he had a point.

"Okay," Nate conceded. "But if you hear anything, you let me know, okay?"

"Yeah, no problem," Tre laughed. Something about the laugh made Nate shudder.

The Saint Patrick's Day Parade in South Boston was almost as big a deal as Christmas. For hours the sidewalks overflowed with merry makers, and the air was filled with the sounds of bagpipes and marching bands. Everyone from the various school groups and local politicians to veterans' associations and policemen had their contingents marching proudly. Senator Bulger—the Corrupt Midget, as some newspapers liked to call him—would walk up and down the street for hours, shaking every hand and kissing every baby. And every year—recently anyway—the gay groups had tried to participate too. This year they were allowed to be in the parade, and their supporters would be marching alongside the parade holding signs loudly and proudly reminding everyone they were there. The angry protesters' would be ready as well.

And of course the beer and laughter flowed freely from the time the sun rose. To Patrick, it was more than a day outside when anyone would hand you a beer no matter how young you looked. It was a reminder that the Irish had conquered Boston, once and for all. America had the Fourth of July; Boston had Saint Patrick's Day.

The day began early in Patrick's house, since Shannon and Danielle's dance troupe was always part of the parade, winning a ribbon for their performance nearly every year. That meant Ma had to get up early, do their hair and makeup and help them get into their costumes and shoes. They were off before 7:00, but Patrick stayed behind. He had decided to meet up with Sean and Walsh and walk over together once things got going.

Around 9:00, Patrick drug himself out of bed, got dressed, and ate a bowl of Frosted Flakes. He remembered to put his bowl in the

sink but he left the milk out on the counter as he put on his shoes—
Kelly Green Adidas Gazelles that he had been able to snag in the
back room of Deb and George's corner store, the last pair in his size.
He smiled proudly at them as he grabbed his jacket and left out the
front door. He fought a sick feeling in his stomach when he realized that for the first time ever—PJ wouldn't be joining them. After
walking down to the corner of his street, he turned toward Sean's
house. Ten minutes later he banged on the door.

Sean appeared at the door wearing sweat pants and a tank top.
Patrick immediately noticed a new tattoo on his right pec. It was
an intricately detailed rendition of Notre Dame's mascot—the
Fighting Irish—holding a pistol in each hand. Tats were illegal in
Massachusetts, so Patrick figured he must have ridden his new bike
to Rhode Island.

"Shit," Sean said, clearly surprised that it was already morning.
"Hang on. I'll be right out."

The parade sounds got closer as they walked to Walsh's house, and soon all three of them had joined the throng of emerald-clad partiers. About twenty minutes later, Danielle and Shannon's dance troupe passed, and the boys cheered and whooped extra loud in support. Several times they toasted PJ, and a few times they even allowed themselves to shed a few tears.

The day seemed to go by more quickly than Patrick had remembered in years past. He had spaced out his beers enough so that he was not very drunk by the time he made it back to his street. His mother wouldn't bother him to be in today, he knew. Despite the merrymaking, he felt restless and uneasy. His college applications were finally in, thank God, but he felt very unsure of what came next. He was also very frustrated that Nate hadn't been able to find anything out about his cousin, and he suspected him of holding something back.

But more than anything else, Patrick felt a deep, unrelenting grief at PJ's loss. The day hadn't been the same without him. It was too soon to feel happy by remembering him; it still hurt too much that he wasn't there.

As Patrick drew nearer to his house, the sight of Kiley's bedroom window awakened a different feeling that was a welcome distraction from the absence of his cousin. Her parents might still be out, he thought, but then they might be coming home at any time. Still, he had to try.

He picked up a small pebble and threw it up to the window. In a second, the curtains parted just an inch and he saw her peer out to see who it was. A minute later she was down by the back door. It was dusk, so it was unlikely, but not impossible, that anyone would see him sneak around the side of the house.

"My parents are passed out, and my brothers are at my cousin's house!" Kiley said excitedly. "Come inside!"

Patrick eagerly obeyed, taking off his shoes and carrying them as they snuck upstairs together. They shut her door quietly, and then began kissing and undressing each other on Kiley's twin bed with its pink flowered comforter. Despite her innocent demeanor, she seemed to want him as urgently as he wanted her. Maybe this was what love felt like.

The creaking of the bed seemed loud, only because they both knew her parents were almost directly beneath them, snoring on the living room couch. Still, it made the entire experience more thrilling to know they could get caught at any minute. Patrick mentally prepared to hide under the bed if the need arose.

But in the end, Kiley's parents remained sound asleep, and Patrick lingered in her bed, running his hand over the length of her body and caressing her gently as she rested her cheek on his chest. For those few moments, the pain of PJ's death and the growing uncertainty of his future seemed farther away. Lying there, naked, under a pink comforter, Patrick felt almost at peace.

CHAPTER 15

PATRICK DECIDED TO walk to school on an early April spring morning. The sun glistened and was melting the snow. The fresh scent of season's change was in the air. He entered the cafeteria. Students were either scrambling to get their homework done before first class or having some sort of breakfast. Patrick joined a few other students and began to read the *Boston Herald*, as usual. It was March Madness, so Larosa, an Italian kid from either the North End or East Boston, was running bets on the Final Four tournament at the next table. Students were handing him cash as he handed out carefully prepared squares. Patrick noticed Nate walking towards Larosa's table as Larosa yelled over " Hey Patrick, you want in?" Patrick responded "Sure I'll go with Nate's picks!". Things at school seemed calmer for the first time in weeks.

When Nate finished placing his bet, he sat down at the table next to Patrick. " I picked us a winner! You get to the page yet about all those riots in LA? Crazy shit!" The school bell rang noisily and most of the students gathered up their things and started off to class. As Patrick and Nate headed off to Father O'Connor's class, Andre entered the cafeteria and waved Nate over abruptly—He was sporting a fresh welt on his left eye!

Later that day, when the lunch bell sounded and the students were walking in and out of the building from the schoolyard courts, the sound of a helicopter rang loudly in the air. It sounded like it was about to land on the school. The students were looking up but couldn't see a thing. It could have been the Boston City Hospital helicopter, but it never sounded this close before. Patrick was sitting on the wall of the court when Walsh rode up on his bike cautiously. Patrick was nervous. What news would his friend Walsh bring this time? Nate and Andre were still shooting on the court as the students poured out and looked up in the air.

Mayor Ray Flynn trying to resolve racial tensions during a riot just prior to being hit in the neck by a bottle and sent to the Hospital.

Walsh said, "This shit is insane! There was a riot up Southie High and Mayor Flynn got hit in the neck with a bottle! The chopper is just circling around the Heights—hundreds of cops are there. As soon as it started this morning I got out of there fast. Then an hour ago, I heard some kids from the neighborhood were coming over here with bats and chains." The schoolyard crowd had grown larger and more segregated by the minute. Patrick noticed Nate in the middle of a large group of rowdy black kids. He knew that one push, one comment would be the match on the gasoline.

Nate stepped out of his crowd and motioned to Patrick as the chopper vibrated loudly. Students and priests looked out of the windows with fear and concern for what the next few moments would bring. Nate and Patrick met halfway out from their crowds. Time was standing still for the moment. Nate put his hands up—"Looks like there's about to be another Boston Massacre. Andre said this has been brewing since this morning, some scrap happened in the gym. Then the riot, the mayor—now there's threats of some Southie and Dorchester kids on their way over here with weapons. Look man, the Cathedral projects are right there. He pointed to the large, predominately black housing projects adjacent to the back of the Cathedral. Those brothers are ready. They're surrounding this school right now.

Patrick was unsure of what to do. He knew Nate was confused, nervous, and outnumbered. As he looked up, he saw Father Lydon's eyes looking down on him from the window. Patrick's dad had him in the ring those very early years of his life—he was no stranger to fighting in the ring, or in the streets. He always remembered his dad saying, "Fighting is the way men can resolve their differences respectably with their hands, one on one!" Even though Patrick's heart was filled with anger and vengeance, he knew this was not right.

He was exhausted and stuck. Unconsciously, he put his hand out to shake Nate's hand. Caught by surprise, Nate hesitantly shook, while dozens of Boston Police Department squad cars arrived to secure the inevitable riot from exploding.

CHAPTER 16

"**N**ATE!" HIS MOM yelled furiously as she walked through the door after her shift.

"Yes, Mom?" Nate said, looking up from his chemistry book where he sat studying at their little table. He immediately decided to say nothing about the school day.

"Your cousin Tremont has been arrested. They found a kilo of raw cocaine in his backpack! Aunt Carol is at the station now, but they've set the bail at something ridiculous. Even with a bond, she can't afford it. And this Sunday is Easter!"

"What?!" Nate's stomach leaped to this throat, and he thought he might vomit. What the hell had Tre been thinking letting Ricky use him as a mule?! The stupidest drug pusher on the planet knew that being busted with that much product on you meant intent to distribute and an eternity in jail. But his thoughts quickly jumped to his own situation and Mom's wrath.

"Did you know anything about this, young man?" Mom demanded.

"No, ma'am," Nate replied, trying his best to meet her penetrating gaze. He could feel his heart rate increase and his palms dampen with sweat.

"You are a terrible liar, Nate. After all these years do you think I can't tell when my own son is lying to me?" she demanded.

"Mom! Tre is 19! Do you think he tells me everything he does? I hardly see him or Slugs—I mean Alvin—these days! I'm at school, or I'm at practice. I'm not a thug!"

"I never said you were a thug," she corrected him, looking into his eyes. "But I'm asking you if you knew your cousin Tremont—MY SISTER'S SON AND TROY'S LITTLE BROTHER—was involved in selling that demonic rock out there." She gestured toward the window. "And you are saying no, you didn't, and I am telling you that you are lying to me. Now go to your room!"

Nate obeyed, picking up his chemistry book and walked angrily to his room. He wanted more than anything to stay and argue with her. He wanted to remind Mom that she had just asked if he knew anything "about this," which could have meant the arrest, not Tre's general involvement with drug dealing. He wanted to point out that he couldn't be held responsible for Tre's actions. That Tre had always been the most volatile of the three cousins, and that everyone knew he had become more and more unpredictable since his brother's death.

But he said nothing. There was nothing he could say that would make his mother see the situation from his perspective. She saw the world in black and white, right and wrong. If you stuck to the right path, you'd probably be okay. Sure, tragedies like Troy's death happened, but there was nothing you could do about that. But if you strayed from the right path, God help you, you would be struck down, sooner or later. That's just the way it was.

Nate tried to refocus on molarity and molality and all the other concepts that he knew would appear on the upcoming chemistry exam, but all he could think about was Tre. Was he wearing the orange jumpsuit already? Was he scared? How long would he be locked up?

And despite his frustration with his mother, he did feel guilty for not saying anything when Tre and Slugs first came to him with their stupid scheme. But, really, what difference would it have made? His mom would have told Aunt Carol, and she would have intervened, maybe. But she worked all the time. What could she possibly be able to do to control her grown son's behavior at this point?

Nothing. Without Troy watching over them, Tre and Slugs did whatever they wanted.

"Hey, Kiley told me to give you this," Shannon said, handing Patrick a piece of lined paper folded over several times into a small triangle. Students—mostly girls—passed notes folded that way to each other all the time.

"Thanks," Patrick said, taking it from her and putting it into his pocket. He wasn't going to read it in front of his sister, whatever it said, although he figured that Shannon had probably read it already. You could never trust little sisters not to snoop if the opportunity presented itself.

Just then, Ma came through the door carrying a bucket of fried chicken and fish from the Fish Pier.

"Dinner!" she yelled, as she slammed the door behind her and walked into the kitchen. "Goddamn it, Paddy, is it too much to ask for you guys to clear the table before I get home?" Patrick said nothing, but helped her move the papers and dirty dishes off the table and onto the counter so there was room for the food.

Shannon appeared first and went to the cabinet to put out the plates and cups, and then Danielle followed with the silverware. Soon they were sitting around the table, chewing in silence.

"So how was school, girls?" Ma asked, taking a sip of her iced tea.

"Fine," Danielle said distantly, admiring her own fingernails, which she had just painted.

"I got a hundred percent in math!" Shannon said excitedly.

"That's my little genius!" Ma said, pleased. For a moment, Patrick wished he could be in fifth grade again, when Ma said those things to him, and life seemed so straightforward and simple. Suddenly, he remembered something Father Lydon had said to him at school the other day.

"Ma, you mailed off those financial aid forms for college right?"

"What forms?" Ma seemed to have no idea what he was talking about.

"Are you serious, Ma?" Patrick said in disbelief. "I gave you those forms like before Thanksgiving break. How the hell long could they possibly take?" The living room was open to the dining area in the kitchen, so he got up and took a few short steps to the to the stack of bills and other papers on the little table by the large armchair. He felt his sisters' and mother's eyes on him as he shuffled through the stack. There, toward the bottom, were the financial aid forms that Father Lydon warned him were due a month ago.

"Ma," Patrick said as he grabbed the papers, a surge of anxiety overwhelming him. "These were really, really important!"

"Well I'm sorry, you ungrateful brat!" she shrieked back at him, lighting a cigarette between her shaking fingers. "I had to do the god-damned income taxes. I'm sorry I've been so goddamn busy working all the time to keep food on the table, this roof over your head, and those fifty dollar Girbaud jeans I got you from Jones' that you're wearing on your sorry, ungrateful ass! Your no-good daddy has been gone ten years and have you ever needed anything that I didn't provide you?"

Patrick was silent in response. He was furious, frustrated, and tongue-tied. Shannon and Danielle finished their food, cleared their dishes, and left the room. You didn't want to get caught in Mom's crossfire when she was on a rampage.

"That's goddamn right, you haven't!" she screamed. "But now I'm supposed to apologize to you because I forgot some goddamn forms you gave me six months ago and never mentioned since. Well, I'm sorry you pathetic..."

That was enough for Patrick. He got up from the table without looking at his mother, walked out the front door and slammed it behind him. It was getting dark, and he started walking to the corner at a deliberate pace, not sure exactly where he was headed. The night air was cool and he could feel tears of rage drying on his cheeks. Of course he should have remembered about the forms too. Father Lydon had emphasized it several times. And of course his mother had done a good job taking care of him and his sisters. He had no right to complain about how his life had gone so far.

But on the other hand, she was his mother. Was it so much to expect her to know what she was doing and help him figure out his future? That question got closer to the resentment he was feeling. He thought back to the *carpe diem* movie, *Dead Poet's Society*, which he had seen last year. There, in an elite private boys school, all the characters had resented the expectations that society and their parents had for them. Neil, a character who discovered he loved acting, committed suicide rather than submit to his father's desire for him to go to Harvard and become a doctor. The movie had made it seem like the entire world was telling you exactly what to do, and it was your job to resist and follow your own voice.

Patrick's thoughts drifted to Nate, with his mother constantly hounding him about grades, basketball and college preparation. Nate wasn't a likely candidate for suicide, he thought, but Patrick knew Nate bristled under his mother's orders and the rigid structure she demanded for his life. He had so much more freedom than Nate had, but maybe that wasn't all it was cracked up to be.

Both Neil—a fictional, rich white kid—and Nate had clear paths

charted for them by the adults in their lives. They might have preferred to have a little more say in the matter, but at least they had
somewhere to start. Patrick felt like he had to figure out everything
for himself, and despite Father Lydon's attempts to guide him—
sometimes, he just wanted someone else to take charge of things.

Patrick looked up to see where he was, and was surprised at how
quickly he had been walking in his anger. He was almost at Sean's
house, as if he had come there on autopilot. He knocked on the door.
Sean's dad had died in a car accident four years earlier and his mom
was on disability, and spent most of her time in bed watching soap
operas, so Sean had always been able to come and go as he pleased.

"What's up?" Sean asked, coming out onto the stoop and sitting
down. He offered Patrick a cigarette and a light, which he accepted.

"Nothing, except my stupid ma forgot to fill out my financial aid
forms, so now I might not get to go to college after all." Patrick took
a drag on his cigarette and blew the smoke out slowly. The sun had
completely set now, and the streetlights were on.

"Screw college. You need to come over and work with me," Sean
said, patting him on the back. "I started out running errands at Triple
O's," Sean was hesitant to say the name, but Patrick knew what
working at Triple O's meant, "and they were paying me three times
what I was making as a bus boy. Now the cash I'm making is unbe-
lievable." Sean wouldn't say exactly where that cash was coming from,
but Patrick knew he was smart to be careful. Five years ago, some
young guy had bragged about dealing drugs for Whitey after a few
beers at a barbeque; his body had washed up on the beach a couple
of weeks later. The death was ruled a suicide.

"Yeah?" Patrick asked. "What kind of work is that?" He knew
Sean couldn't really answer the question, but his curiosity was still
aroused. Up to this point, Sean had been entirely tight-lipped with
him and Walsh about his activities.

Whitey Buger and his Irish Mob's bar on West Broadway–aka "The Bucket of Blood"

"A little of this and a little of that. My operations are expanding, and my skills are finally being recognized." Self-satisfaction oozed from Sean's voice, and Patrick was intrigued. It sounded like he was talking about drugs, of course, which Patrick had no interest in. But still, if college really wasn't meant to be, maybe he shouldn't dismiss Sean's offer so lightly.

"Anyway, you just do whatever you need to do. Things have a way of working themselves out," Sean assured him.

Calmed by the cigarettes and the conversation, Patrick headed home. Sean was right. Things would work out. He could always get a regular job for a year and try for college again after that. He didn't think he'd go into organized crime the way Sean had, but there were other options. He could be a fireman, get into a union or take the cadet test. He could work at a bar. They made pretty good money and it was in cash.

Soon, he was back on his street passing Kiley's house, and suddenly remembered her note. It was dark, which meant her parents were in bed, but he saw a dim light in her room, which might have been a nightlight. He crossed the street to her house and again threw a piece of gravel up to her window. Sure enough, the curtains parted and her face appeared. Like clockwork, she was at the back door of her house, opening it as quietly as she could.

"Oh my God!" she whispered, grabbing him around the waist and burying her face in his chest.

"What's wrong?" he asked, trying to pull away enough to see her face. She opened her mouth to speak, but started to cry. "It's okay, you can tell me."

"Patrick," she said, trying to force the words out. "I think I'm pregnant."

CHAPTER 17

"**S**HIT, I'M SORRY," Nate offered sincerely. Neither spoke for a moment. "Are you sure it's yours?"

"Definitely," Patrick said sulkily. "I was definitely her first, and I'm pretty sure there hasn't been anyone else. She's not that type."

"What are you going to do?"

"Damned if I know," Patrick answered. How could he be so stupid and naïve? Of course Kiley wouldn't know anything about birth control the way his other girlfriends had. How could he have not thought about that? He wasn't ready to join the carriage race like so many others had by 16 or 17. "So you don't know nothing about this stuff?"

"Have I ever gotten anyone pregnant?" Nate asked, raising his eyebrows. "No, I haven't. My mom threatened to cut it off if I did, so I have been pretty damn careful on that front, if I do say so myself."

"Yeah, somehow that doesn't surprise me," Patrick laughed. "Do you think I should have her get rid of it?"

"I thought you guys didn't do that," Nate said, surprised.

"What do you mean, 'us guys'?"

"Like Catholics or whatever," Nate explained.

Patrick shrugged his shoulders. "Some do, some don't. Damned if I understand it. I mean, I guess it's up to her, but shit, how's she gonna keep it? She's a sophomore in high school."

"Well, she might have an aunt or someone who could raise it for her. Then I don't think you'd have to pay anything, as long as someone else adopts it and takes responsibility."

Somehow Nate was always able to think practically, no matter what the situation. That might have pissed Patrick off when it came to college applications, but in this case, he appreciated it. That was exactly what he needed right now. Someone to help him think through the contingency plans.

"Jesus, what should I do?" Patrick asked.

"Well, is she really sure? Like has she been to the doctor or did she just miss her...her..." Nate trailed off. Neither boy felt like discussing the intricate details of the female reproductive cycle.

"I don't know," Patrick admitted.

"Well, find that out first," Nate advised. "I mean, no sense in making plans if she's just a little late."

"How do we find out for sure?" Patrick asked.

"Well she's got to go to the doctor or take one of those home tests," Nate said thoughtfully. "But maybe don't buy it on your side of town where people would know either. Honestly, just come buy one at the drug store near me. You'll be the only white kid in there, but no one will know who you are."

"Okay. I'm not gonna get shot there like my cousin?" Patrick was mostly joking. But not completely.

"Not if you come during the day," Nate promised. "I'll go with you if you want."

"So you really never found out nothing about PJ?" Patrick asked, wanting to think about something else for a while.

"I swear, I asked everyone I could think of. My friend who pushes for Castle Gate honestly knew nothing. My cousin Tre just went off about Troy dying again. The cops just take so damn long to show up when something happens, especially after dark."

"Does Tre bang?" Patrick asked.

"Sort of," Nate sighed. "He just got locked up for possession with intent to distribute. He rolls with some up and coming crew called the Norfolk Kings. They've been trying to move a little product on the edge of Castle Gate territory. But they're small time, trust me. Just wannabes at this point."

"Ugh," Patrick sighed, frustrated again. "Sorry he's locked up, though."

"Me too, but it's his own goddamned fault," Nate lamented, shaking his head. "I told him this would happen as soon as he told me his little scheme. You know they caught him with a full ki? Rodney—the guy I know who pushes for Castle—he'd never be caught with more than four vials. That way they can't get you for dealing, just potentially using. Rodney makes all his little runs to the houses where they store product. He probably walks 30 miles a day. And they move the stuff all the time so the narcs can't find it. Besides, Rodney's still only a junior like me."

"What difference does that make?"

"He's 17, so he's still a minor," Nate explained. "If he gets caught, especially with no record, he might get off easier. Trust me, they use even smaller kids when they can, especially to move a lot of weight from one safe house to another. It's disgusting."

"Huh," Patrick said. A vague thought began to form in his mind that he was afraid to ponder.

"Anyway, I'm sad about Tre, but I'm more worried for his brother. Slugs is not a bad kid, he's just kind of stupid and follows what Tre does, especially after what happened to Troy," Nate sighed. "I'm afraid he's right behind Tre."

"Hey," Patrick said, a new thought suddenly occurring to him. "I have another question."

"Sure."

"My mother forgot to fill out my financial aid forms for college. I got into Suffolk, but it's too much to pay without any aid. Father Lydon was sure I'd be eligible, but we just sort of forgot about the forms." It was painful for Patrick to admit that Nate's nagging about importance of deadlines had been valid. But it was also a relief to get this other problem off his chest.

"Tell your mom to fill them out anyway," Nate said confidently. "There's no guarantee it will work, but if you don't turn them in, you'll definitely get nothing."

"That's a good way to look at it," Patrick conceded. "But my ma and I already fought about it. I don't know if she'll..."

"Apologize to her, and sit with her while she does it," Nate advised. "I'm serious. Those people in charge of the college money, they can do whatever the hell they want. Sure, they have the right to deny you, cause you missed the deadline. But they can still give it to you if they want to. You'll never know unless you ask."

CHAPTER 18

PATRICK WOKE UP the morning of graduation in a state of near euphoria. Just a week ago his life felt like it was falling apart. Today, he felt on top of the world.

The ceremony would be held at the cathedral where he attended Mass, and everyone would be there. Patrick was the oldest cousin, and so the first of his generation, to graduate from high school and the first in his family to attend college. Tonight, everyone would gather at his house for a party that would celebrate his achievements and his future. The ache that PJ wouldn't be there was still ever-present, but it felt just a little more bearable today.

The weather was sunny and gorgeous. The temperature had risen into the sixties by the time he left for the cathedral, but the air was still crisp and fresh. This was Boston at its most beautiful.

The ceremony didn't feel very long; there were only about two hundred in the graduating class, so the names didn't take too long to read. The class president and the valedictorian gave speeches recounting the highlights of their four years together. Years that Patrick finally felt like he could look back on fondly.

Patrick couldn't help but wonder about what it would be like next year when Nate and the handful of other black juniors were set to graduate with the class. All of them were working as ushers today, perhaps to help let families get used to the idea. Would the mood be as peaceful when they walked across the stage next May?

Finally, Father Lydon took the stage to give the last speech and the benediction:

"Class of 1991: Today's ceremony is the culmination of four years of hard work and God's grace. For most of you, it has involved many late nights of studying when you could have been sleeping. It is not easy to take care of your responsibilities while everyone else around you seems to be living for the moment, but that is exactly what our Heavenly Father asks us to do. Paul's letter to the Corinthians reminds us that God's grace is sufficient for whatever trial or suffering we face. And I know many of you felt like you were relying on His grace during Father Connelly's math exams!"

Many of the students laughed in spite of themselves. Patrick looked proudly at all the friends and family in the church. As he suspected, Walsh and Sean hadn't made it; they had almost certainly slept in. But almost all of his relatives that had been there for PJ's funeral had returned to watch him on his big day.

"Some of you will join the work force upon graduation, but I'm proud to say that a record number of our Cathedral High School graduates will be continuing their education at various four-year colleges and universities around the country." Patrick's heart swelled with pride knowing he was among that number. *"We have always been and will always be Men for Others, so I commission you to depart to serve the world with your gifts and skills."*

There was thunderous applause. The graduates, once outside, flung their caps in the air.

"It's been real, Paddy," Slick said, slapping Patrick on the back and moving on to where his family was gathered in one of the pews.

Next came Patrick's mother, Nana, his sisters, along with countless relatives and neighbors. PJ's parents were there, and he noticed his aunt's eyes were red from crying. PJ would never have a day like this, but Patrick liked to imagine him looking down from heaven and enjoying the moment with him.

"Congrats, man," Nate said, shaking his hand firmly.

"Thanks!" Patrick said sincerely. "Feels pretty awesome, I gotta admit."

"So whatever happened with the financial aid?"

"You were right, man," Patrick admitted. "My mom filled out the forms and turned them in, and they gave me a grant, even though we turned them in over a month late."

"That's awesome, man," Nate said. "I'm really glad to hear it. And Kiley?"

"False alarm, if you can believe it," Patrick said, still unable to fully comprehend his good fortune. Patrick had slipped her the home pregnancy test after dark one night, and Kiley had sent him a note the next day that all was well. Patrick vowed to himself to use condoms from then on, feeling he'd just narrowly escaped punishment for his sins.

"Hey, hey! So the luck of the Irish is real!" Nate laughed.

"Something like that," Patrick said, laughing too. In the mist of his joy, he realized that the unlikely friend in front of him had played no small role in helping him navigate two of the most harrowing ordeals of his young life. Walsh, Sean and PJ—God rest his soul—would always be his boys. But Nate had come through for him and offered wisdom and calm that none of them would have been able to give. Patrick felt genuine appreciation in his heart.

"Hey," Patrick said, an idea occurring to him. "I've got a few hours to kill before the party starts at my house. You wanna go somewhere? Grab something to eat or something like that?"

"You don't want to cool it with Slick and them?" Nate asked. The two had never spent time together outside school or the weight room before.

"Nah," Patrick said. "They'll all be at the party tonight anyway." He thought briefly that it might be rude not to invite Nate to join them that night, but Nate didn't seem offended. Nate probably didn't want to come to Southie any more than he would want to visit him in his part of Dorchester.

Nate thought about the invitation for a moment. He had told his mom he would come right home after the ceremony was over, but it had finished more quickly than either of them had expected. He guessed he had about 90 minutes before she started questioning his whereabouts. Also nagging him was the phone call he had gotten from Slugs that morning, telling him he needed to talk to him as soon as possible.

Slugs almost never called anyone on the phone, which meant that this was probably something big. He had sounded strange and scared, and not in a good way. Nate was sick to death of his routine, and an hour doing something different was not unappealing. Slugs could wait an hour.

"Sure," Nate agreed. "I got a little while before I gotta be back. Where you wanna go?"

Where could the two of them go where one of them wouldn't be shunned? That was a real question, but one Patrick knew the answer to immediately. He motioned for Nate to follow him, and a few short blocks later they were in Chinatown. Nate liked Chinatown, although he rarely went. It was like being in a foreign country, with the strange, incomprehensible signs, the loud garment factories and the endless shops, stands and restaurants crammed on top of each other. After surveying several colorful awnings with gold lettering, they entered a restaurant that looked reasonably clean.

A bell attached to the door rang as the boys entered a tiny dining room, empty except for a man in a white undershirt, drawstring pants, and sandals. He was seated at a back table, cleaning a huge bag of green beans and putting them to soak in a large pot of water. He motioned for them to take any table, so they sat by the front window.

As the man brought them two menus, the boys noticed two large Chinese characters tattooed on his forearm. The detail was incredible; they looked like they had been painted on with a brush. The man took their order in broken English, yelled something in Chinese to someone in the kitchen, and returned to his bag of beans.

Seven minutes later, the boys were eating sweet and sour pork, lo mien and fried rice. The man had laughed at Patrick's obviously fake ID, but brought out two bottles of beer nonetheless. You could get anything you wanted in Chinatown.

Nate—knowing his mother would smell him like she always did—sipped the beer gingerly, drinking less than an ounce or two in total. "What did you think of the ceremony?" Patrick asked, downing his in a few swallows.

"It was good. That verse that Father Lydon shared in the beginning of his speech. My pastor talks about that one a lot."

"What verse?" Patrick asked. He had been to the church religion classes as a child and taken his first communion, but he didn't really know any individual verses of the Bible by heart.

"It's Second Corinthians 12:9," Nate clarified. 'My grace is sufficient for you.' Like how whatever we go through, God's grace will be enough to get through it."

"Huh, I like that," Patrick said. Was it God's grace that had allowed him to get the financial aid and caused Kiley not to be pregnant? Would God's grace help him find PJ's killer? Was that how it even worked?

The food was greasy and delicious, and they finished it quickly. When the man came to collect their plates, Patrick pointed to his tattoo. "Where'd you get that?"

The man laughed and nodded toward the kitchen. "My cook do it. You want?"

"Maybe," Patrick said. The man took the dishes and went to the kitchen, and Patrick looked at Nate. "What do you think? Want some ink today?"

Nate was thoughtful. "When Troy died, my cousins and I talked about getting matching tattoos to remember him. But we never did it," he said. What *had* they done to remember Troy, he wondered. What would Troy want them to do?

Patrick thought about talking to Sean and Walsh about getting matching tats to remember PJ. But he felt the urge to do something now.

"Why don't we both do it? You get one for Troy and I'll get one for PJ. Beats trying to get a ride to Rhode Island," Patrick said.

"I'm not sure," Nate said doubtfully. "Mom is a strictly no-tat woman. Plus I heard you can get diseases if the needle isn't clean." The restaurant was decent enough, but that hardly made it a doctor's office.

"Oh, c'mon!" Patrick said, in disbelief. "You're a grown man now. You can't let that woman dictate every little bit of your life. Let's just go back and check it out." Nate hesitated, but they paid the check and agreed to follow the man back into the kitchen. It was small for a restaurant kitchen, and full of mismatched woks, pots and utensils. It smelled of meat, grease, garlic and soy sauce. They followed the man to a door in the back, which revealed a room lit by a few bright light bulbs hanging from wires in the ceiling. Two walls of the room were covered in shelves, full of bags of rice and noodles and other dry goods neither boy recognized. Against the third wall was a long metal table with needles and inks and a couple of stools in front.

The cook came in a second later, and motioned for them to take a seat. Nate wondered for a minute if this guy knew how to do tattoos that black people would get, but of course he would. He knew people with tattoos of their children's birthdates, death dates of their children, and, of course, sports teams and a million variations of gang names and logos. Really skilled artists could tattoo someone's face on you just like a photograph. Nate thought about Troy and wondered if he had a photo of him.

Of course there was the issue of marking his flesh, something his mother told him the Bible forbade. Nate knew some churchgoers with tattoos, of course, and he knew some fraternities even branded their members. His mother had condemned the brands as willing themselves back into slavery, and Nate saw her point. He could never imagine having his flesh burned like that, but a tattoo...

The cook handed Nate and Patrick a notebook full of sketches, which they assumed were images he had done previously. There were all sorts of Chinese characters and pictures of pagodas and dragons, but also Celtic crosses, Harley Davidson logos, and endless sports mascots. One jumped out at both of them: "Romans 12:19" in ornate calligraphy.

"Woah," Patrick said, recognizing it as a Bible verse. "Wasn't that the one Father Lydon read?"

"No, this one is different. That was Corinthians. This is Romans. It goes 'Vengeance is mine, saith the Lord,'" Nate explained.

"Vengeance is mine" Patrick said, thoughtfully. *Vengeance is mine...justice for PJ...* that's the one. Your mom can hardly get mad if you get a Bible verse, right?"

Nate went through the risks in his head, as he had conditioned himself to do his whole life. No one here knew him nor did they care who he was. Word would never get back to his mother that he had been inside this establishment; the worlds were too disconnected. He could get the tattoo somewhere a little discreet, in small letters, where his mother wouldn't notice.

"Well, I'm getting it," Patrick said, pointing to the picture and motioning his choice to the cook. "Hey, man, why not just do it?"

Nate thought for almost a full minute before he answered. "Nah, man. You enjoy yourself. Thanks for lunch and everything, and congratulations again. I've really got to be heading back."

CHAPTER 19

Suffolk County Jail, August 1991

"Yo, Prospect!" Mo's voice sounded almost friendly.

"Hey, man," Patrick answered. The neighborhood lines were just as stark in prison as they were on the outside. But with everyone—whites, blacks, Asians and Latinos—crammed into one building, some interaction was unavoidable.

Life in prison had gradually improved over the last month, and Patrick was no longer the freshest meat in the pen. Two newer kids, just barely over 18 , had been arrested for arson and armed robbery, and were busy getting the brunt of the beatings and jeers. Patrick had been sized up, as he knew he would be, and had finally passed the test. He was grateful things were better, but he knew he was far from out of the woods. One wrong word or move and he would be right back in the line of fire.

Patrick was just beginning to decode the web of nicknames and put them with faces and reasons. Most were ironic: Baby Boy was enormous, Giggles scowled all the time, and Rico was Italian, not Puerto Rican. He knew that Mo was short for Motown, but Mo was not actually from Detroit. It had all seemed incomprehensible at first, but now it almost made sense.

He was settling in to his own nickname too. "Prospect" wasn't so bad. It meant he had potential, he told himself. His sentence was only five years, with a chance for parole in three with good behavior. Maybe his dreams weren't dead after all.

CHAPTER 20

May 1991

PATRICK LOOKED AT his watch. It was almost 1:30 a.m. His party was still going on at his house, but he, Sean and Walsh had ducked out for some fresh air out onto Broadway. It was late, and he'd had plenty to drink. But it was graduation night. Time to celebrate and forget common sense for just a little bit.

"So what the hell you do for all that money?" Walsh asked, as Sean put his roll of twenties away.

"You know I can't talk about that, shithead," Sean answered, rolling his eyes. "You should be grateful at least one of us is doing something with his life. I mean Paddy here may go to college, but what're you gonna do Walsh? At least PJ was trying to make some moves."

Even with the thickness of his buzz, Patrick was startled by the reference to PJ. So Sean *had* begun to involve PJ in whatever he had going on. He thought back to his conversation with Nate about using minors as drug mules, and wondered vaguely if Sean had just been getting PJ to do his dirty work for him, even if it was just a couple bags of weed or something stupid like that.

The three boys were being loud, especially considering the hour, and they made no effort to move aside as four Chinese guys were huddled around a phone booth. The sidewalk wasn't wide enough for them to pass without someone moving out of the way. Just as they were about to collide, Sean stepped in front of Walsh and elbowed the two closest boys into the street. Sean, Walsh and Patrick kept walking and turned the corner onto C Street.

A few moments later a car pulled up and the four Asians from the phone booth jumped out "Hey," one of the Chinese teens shouted after them. The three boys turned and saw that all four teens had stopped and were pulling antennas off the surrounding parked cars. They swished them menacingly through the air as the teens moved toward them.

"Oh shit," Walsh said, turning to run. "Those things are gonna hurt."

Sean grabbed Walsh by the collar and yanked him close. "We're not getting chased out of the D Street projects, our own damn neighborhood, by any goddamn ch*nks! We're gonna stay right here and whip their sorry asses."

Sean's short speech had used up the tiny window of time they had to flee their attackers. The four teens were nearly upon them, swinging the antennas and speaking to each other in low whispers. Thinking fast, Patrick spotted a dumpster to his left, up against the nearest building. He threw open the top and pulled out a clothes iron, a shower curtain rod and a few glass bottles, which he threw to Walsh and Sean.

A second later the Chinese teenagers were on top of them. Walsh was knocked to the ground immediately by one wearing a red T-shirt, which caused the bottle in Walsh's hand to break in half. He screamed as the kid whipped him mercilessly with an antenna. At the same time, Sean and Patrick charged the other three, Sean breaking a bottle against the face of one and Patrick ramming the iron into the ribs of another. The fourth, whose head was shaved, kicked Patrick skillfully in the back of the knee, causing him to lose balance, and soon the two of them were wrestling and punching each other, rolling all over the sidewalk.

Patrick lost sight of what was happening to Sean and Walsh until he gained the upper hand over the bald guy. He could see Sean swinging the curtain rod at one teen, while another got ready to charge him from behind. Patrick was about to shout a warning when he saw a horrifying sight. Walsh was struggling to get up from under the guy in the red shirt, but the young man was bleeding heavily from the abdomen, where Walsh had stabbed him with the broken bottle. His shirt was soaking wet, and blood was quickly pooling on the sidewalk.

Just then all seven boys heard the sound of cop sirens approaching. "5-O, 5-O!!!" shouted Patrick urgently. He, Walsh and Sean rose and fled in separate directions, while two of the Chinese did the same. Patrick looked back briefly and saw that a police car had pulled up to the scene of the fight and that the boy Walsh had stabbed wasn't moving. To his horror, he locked eyes with a black cop, who saw him and immediately took off after him.

Patrick ran as fast as he could, breathing hard. His calves and quads began to burn, but he willed himself to accelerate. He squeezed through a chain link fence and jumped down onto the old Amtrak tracks. While he caught his breath, he thought he was home free. A second later, he was pinned to the pavement, the cop on top of him, cuffing his hands behind him. He felt the air forced out of his lungs as the cop kneeled on him, pressing the full weight of his body into Patrick's back for what seemed like an eternity. His eyes were going dark and he thought he tasted blood in his mouth. The cop finally stepped off of him and he gasped for breath.

The cop grabbed Patrick's head by the hair, pulled it up, and slammed it back into the tracks. Pain shot through his entire skull, and he thought he might vomit. He felt an open cut on one side of his face and blood begin gushing from his nose. His head throbbed unbearably. Patrick braced himself for another blow. Sure enough, he felt a kick in his side, bruising his ribs and knocking the wind out of him again. Patrick coughed and struggled to breathe.

Finally the cop grabbed the back of his shirt and lifted him to his feet. Rage and hatred surged through him as he met the cop's gaze.

"Who the hell do you think you are?" Patrick gasped, when he had his breath back. "Do you know Sergeant Daly?" He stared directly into the cop's eyes when he said it. He was sure he saw the cop flinch.

"Get in the car," the cop said, his loathing obvious.

"You'd better let me go," Patrick warned him, spitting on the ground defiantly.

"You have the right to remain silent," the cop answered. "Anything you say can be used against you in a court of law. You have the right to an attorney..." the cop continued reading Patrick his Miranda rights before opening the back door of the car and shoving Patrick inside.

"What's the charge?" Patrick demanded.

"The Chinese kid in a coma back there," the cop said, looking at him in the rearview mirror from the front seat. "He might not make it. You know anything about that?"

Patrick said nothing.

"I'll bet you a thousand dollars that's his blood on your jeans," the cop continued. Patrick looked down and noticed an enormous smear of blood on his left pant leg. "You assaulted an officer, and if you don't shut the hell up, I can also prove you were also carrying enough pot to be busted for intent to distribute. You want me to keep going?" The cop held up a large sandwich bag with unrolled weed.

Patrick said nothing. He heard the cop calling the arrest in as they rode to the station, as the reality of his situation began to sink in. How long would it take his mom to find a lawyer and post bail?

At the station he was brought into an interrogation room and placed in a chair. The cop who had arrested him uncuffed his hands and put them into cuffs that were bolted to the table. Then he bent over and did the same with his ankles with cuffs that were bolted into the floor.

"I need a lawyer," Patrick said instinctively.

"We can do that," the cop said with a patronizing smile. "Why don't you wait here for a second and think it over."

He shut the door. Patrick was exhausted. The buzz from the alcohol had worn off and his head and body ached from his beating. He caught a glimpse of himself in the mirror—which he knew was a one-way window that allowed other detectives to watch him while he was interrogated—and saw how bloodied and bruised his face looked.

About five minutes later, Sergeant Daly came in and sat down at the table opposite Patrick.

"What the hell happened to you?" he asked. His voice was low, but he sounded concerned.

"That black cop beat the shit out of me!" Patrick said angrily, expecting the Sergeant to be more outraged.

"Look, I know he roughed you up, but that's the least of your concerns right now. I'm really not supposed to be in here talking to you, but the detective in charge let me in as a favor. Listen, I know you don't want to say who did this, but if you do, I can make sure that no one finds out you said anything. Otherwise, I don't know how you're getting out of here."

"No way!" Patrick exclaimed, outraged that the Sergeant thought he would break the code of silence. "I'm not a rat!"

I don't want to see you to go down like this Paddy! We can keep it from getting out. Look, my brother is in federal prison on RICO

141

charges because he wouldn't rat on Whitey on the last round up by the feds. But that's the underworld bullshit. This is racial shit! Taboo in the courts!

"So you do know who did it," Daly asserted. "Look, I'm telling you, if that kid in the ER dies, they will get you for accessory to murder. The prosecutor might only go for second degree, but still. I know you didn't do it. You'd be covered in his blood if you did. But if you don't tell them what they need to know, I can't protect you from going down for it."

Patrick said nothing and stared into the small radius of himself in the mirror.

———

A few hours earlier, across Dot Ave, Slugs and Nate met on the corner halfway between their apartments. "What'd you need to tell me so bad?" Nate asked impatiently, looking at his watch. His mother would definitely start yelling at him if he wasn't inside in ten minutes.

"You ain't gonna like it, and you can't tell no one," Slugs said, his enormous body starting to shake with emotion.

"Fine, just tell me so I can get home before someone pops us out here or I'm late and Mom kills me her damned self."

"I know who killed your boy. The white boy they found over on Ashmont back in December."

"Shit!" Nate exclaimed. "Who?"

"It was Tre."

CHAPTER 21

ALARGE CROWD OF people gathered on the front steps of the South Boston Courthouse. In spite of the defense attorney's claim that Patrick did not do it, that the Irish boys were acting in self-defense, it was sentencing day for Patrick. In the height of the tension, where the neighborhood lines were shifting more than ever, there was no way in this city at this time anyone would accept this defense. The transport vehicle pulled out and drove parallel to the Courthouse stairs, just long enough for Patrick to peer out the window and see his mother, his little sisters, Kiley and Nana—all in tears. He saw Father Lydon and Father O'Connor, who had testified as character witnesses on his behalf. He even noticed his uncle, his father's brother who he hadn't seen in ten years, speaking to Sergeant Daly. Patrick broke down, immediately overwhelmed with tears and fear.

CHAPTER 22

Suffolk County Jail, September 1991

"**N**ATE!" PATRICK EXCLAIMED, surprised. He had expected it to be his mother, who, along with Walsh, had visited him almost every week since he'd been in. His distress over his own situation hardly compared to the signs of worry on his mother's face. It was as if she had aged ten years in just a couple of days. But instead today he saw his old school friend, wearing a polo shirt and jeans, looking young and healthy.

"Hey, man. Thought I'd drop by and check you out," Nate said, trying to sound casual. He had actually been there to see Tre, but felt like it would be a betrayal not to look in on Patrick as well. They hadn't spoken since their time together on graduation day, and Nate had been tortured every night since his conversation with Slugs about whether he should let Patrick know about Tre's role in PJ's death.

Patrick didn't look as bad as Nate had worried he would. Nate based this on how Tre had looked after he had to prove himself through his brutal initiation. Tre had managed to find protection in a crowd after beating one of the larger inmates, escaping the fight with only a broken nose.

Patrick's bruises and scars had healed up, and he too no longer looked like the abused man at the bottom of the totem pole. He was relieved that Nate hadn't come to see him when he looked much worse.

"So how's it going? You're a senior now, huh?" Patrick asked. It felt good to think about something other than his life inside and his mother's suffering.

"Yeah, man. A lot happening." Nate wasn't trying to be evasive, but he also didn't want to rub Patrick's face in his own successes.

"Like what? College stuff?" Patrick asked.

"Sure. Some schools are interested in me for ball like you said, so we're following through with that," Nate explained, downplaying its importance.

"That's great, man. See, I told ya."

"Thanks," Nate said, a little uneasily. For the first time in his life, he was experiencing the guilt of being better off than many of the people he cared about. When the scholarship offers had first come in, his mother had cried, of course. Nate had felt more relief than anything else. He had finally settled on the University of Virginia, and signing day was in just over a month. Now the reality of the gulf between him and Slugs, and of course Tre, who was locked up, was becoming more real to him. Tre—if he ever got out and got his act together—would struggle for the rest of his life with the ex-con mark on his resume. Slugs was probably headed down the same road.

"Guess it's a little ironic," Patrick laughed. "You always told me you'd end up in here if you sneezed in the wrong direction and here I am, all because I stayed out too late one night."

"Yeah," Nate said. He didn't feel like laughing. "But listen, you didn't do it right? Everyone at school says it was someone else, and you're in here because you won't say who."

"I didn't stab the kid, no," Patrick sighed. He'd been through it a million times in his head. "But the kid who did it, did it in self-defense. But they'll never believe him. If I rat, he'll face manslaughter at least."

Nate shook his head and sighed. He knew it was no use, and he respected Patrick's stand. For the first time he understood his own mother's frustration, watching young people make decisions that seemed loyal and honorable, only to jeopardize their own futures so unnecessarily. Would he, Nate, go to jail to protect Slugs, Tre, or a friend like Andre? It was a hard question he hoped he'd never have to answer.

They talked more about school and a little about girls. Patrick admitted that Kiley had written him three times since he'd been in and he hadn't written back once.

"I don't know what to say," Patrick sighed. "Plus, she'd be better off moving on, don't you think?"

Nate had to admit he had a point. But still, he imagined having a girl waiting for him might help Patrick stay focused on behaving himself and getting out as soon as possible. Maybe Kiley could even persuade him to tell the cops something to get him released earlier.

"Hey, I heard you can take classes in here," Nate said brightly. "You doing anything like that?"

"Naw, not yet," Patrick said dismissively. "The only good thing about this place is it's not school, right?"

"Yeah," Nate agreed. "But still. It could be a good opportunity. At least learn to type or something like that."

CHAPTER 23

June 1992

Patrick's arms were shaking slightly, but he forced the barbell back into its cradle above his head without much trouble. He could now bench press 300 with relative ease and squat even more. He was also part of an informal boxing ring, and had improved both his footwork and his speed immensely. With nothing else to do, he had thrown himself into becoming faster and stronger with a level of self-discipline that had eluded him in high school.

It was almost as if for the first time in his life, he could focus. He had even begun to read a few books, just like Nate had urged. He reread a few novels from English class. The stories seemed more interesting now that he had nothing else to think about. He also thumbed through a business book that someone had donated to the prison library.

None of this made prison bearable. That would be impossible. The food was terrible, the beds were uncomfortable, and Patrick quickly tired of the television shows they were allowed to watch. Sexual assault in the showers was often a reality, although Patrick had managed to escape it, now he was strong and respected enough to be left alone. But as Patrick's first year inside drew to a close, he began thinking about his release with a sense of purpose. He would still be young when he got out. He could go back to school. Maybe he couldn't go into politics as an ex-con, but maybe he could. He could certainly go into business.

"Yo, what up, Prospect?" Mo asked him. Patrick thought Mo's high top fade reminded him of the taller member of the rap/comedy duo Kid n Play.

"Nada," Patrick answered.

"Spot me on bench press?" Mo asked.

"Sure."

Mo finished three sets, more or less in silence and then sat up. The veins in his neck, head and arms bulged with each effort. His eyes looked vacant to Patrick, almost soulless. They reminded him of someone, but he couldn't recall who. "Thanks," Mo said, and wiped his forehead on the sleeve of his jumpsuit. "Hey, I don't think I ever heard what you in for." The two of them had rarely talked outside the weight room, as everyone still kept to their own.

"Wouldn't give up my boy in a stupid brawl with some Chinese. The guy my buddy stabbed died, so it'd be manslaughter for him. I'm just an accessory or whatever. Shoulda run faster, I guess."

Mo nodded his approval.

"What about you?" Patrick ventured.

Mo laughed, almost demonically. "Oh, I've done a lot of shit. But they busted me on intent to distribute. I'll be out soon, no doubt. Unless they find out more than they know now. And if they do, I gotta plan to pin it on someone else!"

Patrick nodded. Mo's words sounded like typical prison *bravado*. Everyone implied they were capable of murder, if for no other reason, to help them survive. But a year inside had given Patrick experience in sizing people up, and he sensed authentic brutality in Mo's voice.

"What school you go to?" Patrick asked.

"Dorchester, class of 1989," Mo said somewhat proudly. Surviving Dorchester High School was something to brag about. "You?"

"Oh, I was a Cathedral boy," Patrick laughed self-deprecatingly, knowing it was less common for a Catholic school kid to end up inside.

"No shit?" Mo responded, surprised. "My cousin went there."

Nate knocked on the rattling screen door as loud as he could without putting a hole through it, wondering if anyone could hear him inside over the blare of the television. He tried three times before Patrick's mom, Kathy, opened the door and stared at him.

"Mrs. Ryan," Nate began, meeting her unfriendly gaze. "I'm sorry to bother you. I just wanted to talk to you about something. It has to do with Patrick."

Kathy stared at him for a moment. Then, without a word, she pushed the screen door open and motioned for him to enter. The house looked filthy to Nate's eyes, and he could smell the stench of cigarettes as soon as he entered the front door. Out of habit, he almost asked if he should remove his shoes, but then thought better of it.

Shannon was parked in front of the television watching "The Fresh Prince of Bel Air". Nate smiled a little to himself as he followed Kathy to the kitchen table. He wondered if anyone in Southie actually believed there were black people who lived in mansions and had butlers, like Will Smith's character did on the show.

"Turn that down!" Kathy commanded, as they both sat down at the table. "So what is it?" she finally asked, staring at him. She sounded exhausted.

"I'm not sure how to explain this," Nate began, "but do you know anything about the Norfolk Kings? They were in the news a little; they're low level gangbangers from Dorchester."

"Maybe," Kathy shrugged. "What the hell does this have to do with Paddy?"

"Two of my cousins' sort of run in that gang. It's complicated. But one is in jail with Patrick. The other one is out. And a while back I found out that..." Nate's voice trailed off. How could he say what he needed to say without completely betraying his family? The last time he visited Tre, Nate learned Tre was scheming up a master plan to pin the murder charge on his brother Slugs temporarily— just enough for him to get out. Tre was talking like Slugs was now in a wheelchair and useless, that he could withstand the heat for a little while! He knew there was no stopping Tre.

"What?" Kathy pressed.

"That the Norfolk Kings might have been involved with what happened to PJ. I wasn't there, but..."

Kathy covered her mouth and began to sob. Nate waited patiently, putting his hand on her shoulder. She didn't lean into him, but she didn't pull her arm away either.

"I'm sorry," Nate offered, when she had quieted down.

"Aren't you going away to college now? You come all the way back here to tell me this?"

"I didn't come in town just for that; I was here anyway helping my mom move—" Nate stopped himself. No need to explain that at long last his mom had gotten her teaching certificate and had been hired as a Kindergarten teacher in Charlottesville. The booster club had quietly helped her find a modest apartment nearby where she could take the bus to work and travel easily to all of Nate's home games when the season started. Nate wasn't sure how the deposit on the apartment had been paid, but it had been.

Nate had borrowed one of the alum's pickup trucks and loaded it with all the earthly possessions they were keeping. It took one after-noon. They gave away everything else to their neighbors. He felt nos-talgic, hugging the people he had grown up with, and promising to come visit. And he felt a twinge of guilt; guilt that he was escaping and leaving them behind. But looking at his mother and thinking of her living there alone, he knew he was doing the right thing.

"So why? Why'd they kill him?" Kathy demanded, shaking with rage and grief, but keeping her voice down to avoid arousing Shannon's curiosity.

"I really don't know the whole story," Nate said carefully. He didn't know how sensitive Patrick's mother would be to learning about the things that PJ had gotten mixed up in. "Apparently PJ was supposed to buy some product—you know, drugs or whatever—from the Kings. But instead—and this is just my cousin talking, okay?—he supposedly tried to steal the drugs or under-pay for them, or something like that."

"PJ wasn't a crackhead," Kathy protested, shaking her head.

"No, no," Nate said. "My cousin said the buy was way more than for a single person. Like it was enough to try to distribute or some-thing. They thought maybe they were trying to step on it and sell it for more in Southie. I know they were expecting someone else, not PJ on a bicycle, maybe he had got lost or used up the money from another deal and was trying to make it up somehow."

"Maybe," Kathy said doubtfully. "But I never thought PJ was into anything like that. Now their friend Sean, on the other hand…" her voice trailed off. It was all too awful to ponder.

"Anyway, my cousin Tre used to be a good kid," Nate continued. "But his older brother died from a stray bullet and ever since then it's like something in him snapped. Couldn't stand to be disrespected, and didn't see any point in trying to do the right thing. After all, his brother never did anything wrong, but he died anyway…"

Nate stopped talking. Kathy was crying again, and he could see she was not at all interested in his family history or the subtle differences between his cousins. No need to explain that when it was clear PJ didn't have the right amount of money, Tre shot him in the leg. She wouldn't care that Tre probably just meant to wound him so he'd show up with the rest of the money. No point in explaining that Tre had unintentionally hit PJ's femoral artery and that he'd already lost too much blood by the time he got to the hospital. Why fill her head with images of her poor nephew lying there, bleeding, screaming, and suffering, while the police and ambulance took forever to come to his aid?

"But what I'm really here to ask you is if you think I should say anything to Patrick," Nate continued. "Back when it happened, I promised him I'd tell him whatever I found out. But he's locked up right now and my cousin and a few other Norfolk Kings are in there too…"

"So you're afraid for your cousin? You wanna protect him?" Kathy demanded, turning angry again.

"No, that's not it," Nate said, struggling to stay patient. "Of course I don't want beef between Tre and anybody. He already screwed up carrying dope for the Kings. What's more, my aunt just said they've got witnesses saying he killed some Puerto Rican kid over shoes or something stupid like that. He's going to have another trial, and if he loses this one, I'm pretty sure he'll be in for life."

"So?" Kathy asked.

"Patrick is up for parole in a little over two years," Nate explained. Why did he have to walk this woman through each step? Were these people incapable of thinking ahead? "If I tell him, he will seek vengeance, and if he starts something with Tre inside, first of all, he might get hurt. But whatever happens, fighting will jeopardize his chances of getting out as soon as possible. Killing him will mean he may never get out. But if I don't tell him what I know, I'll feel like I'm breaking the promise I made him."

Kathy paused, thinking this over. Her weary, stressed out, nicotine-addled mind worked its way through the possibilities. If Paddy found out who did it, there was no question he would flip out and want revenge. He wouldn't be able to control his temper, no matter how much anyone told him to wait and let the law handle it. Whether or not she was willing to admit it, this black boy sitting in front of her was right.

Nate knew he was right. He hadn't really come looking for advice; he had come seeking absolution. He wanted Kathy to tell him that it was okay not to tell Patrick what he knew. He wanted her to be an adult and give him permission to do the right thing.

"Look, I don't know what to tell you," Kathy sighed. "You're right that Paddy will want to get back at whoever did it. But if you don't tell him the truth, I can't promise he'll ever forgive you."

CHAPTER 24

May 1993

"LICENSE AND REGISTRATION please?"

Nate sighed and handed both to the officer who had pulled him over. Nothing like being back in Boston.

"This isn't your car, sir. Who is Carmella Washington?" the officer asked. His tone was cordial but cold.

"My mother," Nate said, wearily. "We have the same last name."

"I didn't ask you that," the officer scolded. "Step out of the car please, sir."

Nate obeyed, and followed the officer's directions, placing his hands on the car and spreading his legs. The officer padded him down, but much more lightly than he had experienced in the past. After he found nothing, Nate waited, heart pounding, to see if he would be let go or if the cop would threaten to plant something on him.

"Okay, sir, you're free to go," the cop said. "Have a good day."

"Thank you, sir," Nate said, his voice betraying no emotion. The officer's treatment told him he had come up in the world. Perhaps he'd never rise far enough not to be pulled over for no reason. Perhaps no black man ever would. But at least he hadn't been slammed into the pavement or groped.

Spending his freshman year of college among students who had been raised in gated communities with tennis and violin lessons should have been an intimidating experience for Nate. And in some ways it had been. The students in his English class discussed authors and books he had never heard of with a kind of pretentious ease affected to impress the professors and one another. But after a few weeks he had settled in and learned how to play the game. He had initially struggled with the reading assignments, which were far longer and more demanding than what he was used to. But his tutor showed him how to skim first and go back and read in more detail. By second semester he had tackled Solzhenitsyn with no problem, and Aristotle with a bit more of a struggle.

Nate was determined not to major in kinesiology or sociology like most other athletes on scholarship did. He wasn't exactly sure what he wanted to do, but he met with his advisor periodically to discuss his options. He thought about everything from accounting to engineering and computer science. He even briefly considered law or social work; part of him really wanted to go back to his hometown and make things better. Save some kids from Troy's fate and the trauma and pain such deaths caused. But then he would remind himself that his first job was to take care of himself and his mother, and Aunt Carol and the others if he could. You had to save your own family before you tried to save the entire world.

First stop was his Aunt Carol's apartment, where he would spend the night in Tre's old bed. Slugs had defied the odds and not gotten arrested. He had, however, been shot and nearly crippled. For now, he was confined to a wheelchair and was slowly beginning to walk again. The two exchanged greetings at the door, and Nate bent over to embrace him.

"So you back to visit the little people, huh?" Slugs asked with a laugh. There was no trace of resentment in his voice.

"Don't even try it," Nate laughed. In a way, it felt good to be back in Dorchester, even with its dangers and sorrowful memories. College was exhausting. Besides class and practice, there was the constant effort required to walk the line between fitting in with his peers and being true to who he really was. Nate had resolved long ago that he would rise on his own terms. He would learn the habits and the skills needed to be successful, but he would never pretend to be someone he wasn't. He would never explain away his mother with her calloused hands or her forced proper speech. He would always be Nate from Dorchester. And Slugs would always be his cousin.

"Hey, I'm finally studying for the GED," Slugs said proudly.

"That's great, man," Nate encouraged him.

"Well I can't do much else while I'm rehabbing, but I can do that," Slugs said. Suddenly it occurred to Nate that Tre's arrest had removed his toxic influence over his little brother. Whatever had snapped in Tre—or been wrong all along, who knew?—had only poisoned Slugs by association. Nate couldn't allow himself to think of his cousin's incarceration as a blessing, but since it had already happened, he welcomed the positive development in Slugs.

"You thought much about what to do after you pass it?" Nate asked.

"Not too much, but Mom says they're always hiring electricians. You can learn to do that at the community college. It ain't too much to go there," Slugs said.

"That's good," Nate nodded approvingly. "You know we'll do what we can too. We got you, Slugs. I ain't getting paid yet, but I got you. We'll figure it out." Nate wanted more than anything to urge Slugs and Aunt Carol to join them in Charlottesville. It was a quiet town. Slugs would be bored out of his mind of course, but there were things to do once you settled in. He had been hiking for the first time with a girl named Vanessa from the track team. She reminded him of Denise Huxtable from "The Cosby Show", both because of how she looked and because her father was a doctor.

Nate looked at his watch. "Hey, I'll be back in a few, okay? I put in to visit County to see Tre."

"Tre's in solitary again," Slugs said, shaking his head. "He can't have no visitors."

"Okay," Nate said. "Well, I got another friend in there. White boy from high school. I'm gonna see him real quick too."

"That's nice of you," Slugs said, approvingly. "See you when you get back."

"So you done with freshman year, huh?" Patrick asked. He was glad for a visitor to help break up the monotonous days. But while Walsh's visits had made him feel like he was keeping up with the outside world, Nate coming by after a year reminded him how much his was missing out on.

"Yup." Nate made no effort to elaborate. Once again, he was instinctively conscious about rubbing his success in anyone else's face.

"So what's it like?" Patrick asked. He couldn't look at Nate without thinking of what might have been. His newfound focus had made him more aware of what he was really capable of when he applied himself. Maybe he really could have had a scholarship for hockey or something like that.

"Well, not gonna lie. It was good. The work was really hard, but when you're an athlete they give you tutors to help you study and stuff. And I got decent playing time as a freshman, so that's always a positive."

"Must be nice," Patrick said. He rolled his eyes just slightly as he said it, but Nate noticed.

"Look, we can talk about something else," Nate said.

"No, I wanna hear more about college. You pledge a frat?" Patrick pressed. He was gliding into full self-pity mode now and wanted to force Nate to admit every detail of his cushy, perfect life.

"Yeah," Nate admitted, telling him the name.

"Never heard of it."

"It's an African American one," Nate explained. "Most of the team is in it. I didn't get a brand or anything though."

"So it's 'African American' now?" Patrick laughed. "You really are a college boy, I guess."

"Whatever." Nate was starting to get annoyed. He felt sorry for Patrick, but his old friend was beginning to test his patience.

"So you finally learn to party? No momma to smell your breath every night. Bet the girls are all over you, big basketball star and all that."

"The honeys are nice," Nate admitted. "And we have parties, but it's not like the white frats. They get wasted and puke everywhere. We mostly dance and stuff. Athletes can't get too messed up during our season or we'll get in trouble." Nate could feel where this conversation was going. He resisted telling Patrick that he liked his classes. They were interesting and challenging, even if they were stressful too. He would have liked to try to explain how Vanessa was different from Betina, not that there was anything wrong with Betina, who would always be his first love. He wanted to tell someone how he was both excited and scared to meet Vanessa's parents, who had been married for 30 years and had a summer house at the beach in North Carolina. But he shared none of that.

"Well, you sure did luck out, didn't you?" Patrick asked, shaking his head.

"What?" Nate's eyes narrowed.

"Oh nothing," Patrick said dismissively. "Just saying, it all worked out real nice for you didn't it?"

"Are you kidding me?" Nate asked in disbelief. "Look, I feel as bad as anyone else that you're in here, but are you really going to sit there and say that I just 'lucked out'?"

"Hey, hey," Patrick said. "I didn't mean anything by it. Lighten up man, I am like a caged animal in here. I'm just an ignorant townie. You're the fancy college boy now. Why don't you tell me how it all works?"

"Okay," Nate said, suppressing his urge to raise his voice and willing himself to be calm. "I'll tell you how it works. After my dad died, my mom worked her ass off at shitty jobs twelve hours a day so I would have a shot at a better life. She saved every penny, wore old clothes, permed her own hair, so that I could go to camps and summer league and when the chance came for me to go to Cathedral, she jumped all over it. She had cleaned Billy Bulger's office a few times years ago and had learned he went to Cathedral, so she randomly sent a letter and asked for a letter of recommendation at least 10-15 times, and he finally did it. And I studied for my classes and the SAT hard enough that UVA thought I could not only make it on their basketball team, but at their school. And so now I am busting my ass at practice, and at tutoring, and in the library, and all the rest of it to prove them right. I don't sleep in—I go to all my classes, Patrick. I go to tutoring, I go to practice, and then I study some more. I can't have a job because I'm on scholarship, so I have to be careful not to eat all my meals before the weekend comes. My mom has a better job now, so she tries to give me spending money, but I don't want to take it, because I want her to have something nice for once in her goddamn life. But sometimes I do, because I want to take my girl—I don't even know if she's mine yet—but I want to take her to a movie. I know my teammates and I are making millions for this school, selling out every game, and I gotta take my mom's hard-earned money to take a rich girl on a cheap date. That's my cushy college life!"

Nate paused for a breath. Patrick stared at him. He knew what Nate was saying was true, and he knew he had no right to resent his friend's success. He was impatient to get out, but the closer his release date got, the more he felt the familiar anxiety of his life before graduation. It was one thing to just focus on getting through each day. Soon, he would have to face the outside world again.

"And you know what your problem is?" Nate continued. "You think that everything is just supposed to work out for you. You think the universe is obligated to roll out the red carpet and show you the way. You think being warm and safe and well-fed and successful is a natural state of being, and that all you have to do is exist, and all that stuff will happen for you. Well that's not how life works for kids like me. We have to fight, and push, and pray, and fight some more or we'll be dead. Sometimes we do everything right and we end up dead anyway. But by all means, if I'm just a lucky dude, please tell me if there is anything I can do to help you."

"I asked you to do one goddamned thing," Patrick said, his demeanor more hardened and cold than it had ever been on his worst day of high school. "I asked you to figure out who killed my cousin. And you couldn't even handle that. So why the hell would I ask you for anything else?"

Nate stared at Patrick in silence, considering what he should do. Nate wanted to tell him, to keep his promise and to get the burden off his own chest. He could see Patrick's hands beginning to tremble with emotion.

"When's your first parole hearing?" Nate finally asked.

"About a year and half," Patrick answered.

Nate took a deep breath. "You just behave yourself until then, and maybe I'll catch you on the outside."

Then he stood up and walked out.

CHAPTER 25

February 1995

PATRICK CHANGED OUT of his jumpsuit and found that his old jeans still fit reasonably well, but his shirt and coat were way too tight. More than three years of weightlifting had transformed his torso from a men's medium into an extra-large. His shoes fit, although he knew already they would be dated when he put them on. The first order of business was definitely going to be getting some new clothes.

For a few weeks now, Patrick had known he would be stepping into a different world. Not just because of the time that had passed, but because the unimaginable seemed to have happened. Rumor had it that Whitey had disappeared.

The day was unseasonably warm, which meant about 40 degrees, and there were no clouds. Patrick stared out the window as his mother drove home and was startled by how different things looked to him. The Quiet Man was gone, replaced by a Starbucks, and another pub was now a Chinese restaurant. They turned onto Telegraph Street, and Patrick was startled to see such a large group of black teenagers walking loudly and laughing all the way up to Southie High.

He hadn't really been gone that long, but the neighborhood lines had moved.

They continued toward home, and Patrick noticed a large crowd gathering outside the funeral home.

"What happened?" Patrick asked his mom.

"Mikey Smith hung himself," his ma said sadly.

"How old was he?" Patrick asked with shock. He remembered Mikey as a bright eyed, exuberant youngster. The idea that he could have been suicidal seemed unfathomable.

"Oh, sixteen or something. More than a dozen others have tried in the last six months. Seven more from Southie OD'ed on heroin. The place is different, Paddy. These new pain pills are everywhere and if you can't afford those, the heroin is like ten bucks a bag. Not sure this would be happening if Whitey was still here. There's more color in the projects than a friggin rainbow these days! "

Patrick was in disbelief. He looked out the window again and noticed how much more subdued the people were. Gone were the boisterous yells and the confident strides of pride. They had been replaced by vacant expressions and listless shuffling, as if there was no purpose or hope. Were people actually depressed that Whitey was gone? Or did they feel betrayed as the rumors about his work as an FBI informant seemed to be validated?

"You heard they elected one of their women," Ma continued, shaking her head. "Damn shame. She's already in trouble for not paying her taxes."

Patrick vaguely remembered some news about a black woman getting elected to the state senate. He knew it was a waste of time to ask his ma how many of the Irish politicians paid their taxes in full. He always enjoyed Nana's stories of how the famous Irish Mayor Curley, "the mayor of the poor" had gone to prison twice during his four terms as the Mayor of Boston. As they drew closer to home, the sights became more familiar, and he was relieved to see some things looked the same.

"Hey, look," his ma said as they pulled in front of the house. "There's something you need to know, because you're going to hear it soon enough anyway." Even though the car was off, she was staring straight ahead at the street instead of turning to look at him.

"What?" Patrick asked. Something in her voice made him uncomfortable.

"That black kid you knew from Cathedral came by the house while you were locked up."

"Nate?" Patrick asked. She couldn't have meant anyone else, but Patrick was surprised to hear her voice sound almost warm. Still, why wouldn't Nate have mentioned that he saw Patrick's mother on one of his two visits to him in jail? "When was that?"

"About two years ago," Ma explained, bracing herself for what she had to say next. "I think he found out something about who killed PJ."

"WHAT?!" Patrick exclaimed, instantly furious. How could Nate have found out and not told him? White hot rage began to surge through his veins. "Vengeance is mine… "

"It seems like it might have been his cousin or his cousin's gang," Ma sighed. "The one that was locked up with you. He was in some gang called the Norfolk Kings."

"Mo?!" Patrick was dumbfounded.

"I don't know. Nate called him Tre or Dre or something."

Patrick sat in the car, as if paralyzed. Mo was Tre? A member of Nate's family—someone he had seen every day for the last three years— had killed his cousin PJ, and Nate hadn't had the balls or decency to even let him know. No wonder he had continued to send letters after their argument last year, trying to make up for his betrayal.

Patrick got out of the car and slammed the door shut.

Just as he reached the front door, he noticed a figure with a cane approach on the sidewalk and pause to speak to his mother, who had stayed in the car. It was Father Lydon. He turned to Patrick and motioned to him to come over. Patrick reflexively obeyed.

"Welcome home, Paddy. We're all really glad you're back." Father Lydon extended his hand as he spoke.

Patrick didn't know how to respond. Part of him was deeply touched that his priest would visit his home on the day he was released from prison, while another part of him suspected that his mother had asked him there in anticipation of the news she had to tell him. Prison had toughened him up, but it had not made him so rebellious that he was going to be rude to a priest, so he shook Father Lydon's hand and said nothing.

"Let's talk, Paddy. Do you want to go inside or do you want to help me finish my morning walk?"

Patrick stood in silence for a moment, and then figured it was pointless to try to argue his way out of a conversation he needed to have anyway.

"We can walk," he said, working hard to keep his voice calm.

"Perfect. It's really a lovely day for this time of year, don't you think?" Father Lydon asked. The two walked down the block toward L Street Beach. The cobalt blue water was dazzling in the sun. Despite all Patrick felt in that moment, Father Lydon was right. It was a beautiful day outside.

After several minutes of walking in silence, Father Lydon finally spoke up. "So I take it your mother has told you about your cousin's murder?"

"Yes." The rage was trying to resurface, but Patrick successfully suppressed it for the moment.

"Well, I understand that you're angry with your friend Nate for not telling you what he knew."

"You're damn right, Father," Patrick said. It was all just too much to deal with on his first day out. "I talked to that goddamned punk in the weight room at least three times a week. He never acted like anything was wrong."

"It is quite possible that Tremont is a sociopath," Father Lydon explained. "Or that his older brother's death traumatized him enough that he lost his ability to empathize with others. We can't be sure. But I think you are right that he feels little or no remorse over what he did. The real question is why do you think your friend Nate didn't tell you?"

"Because he's a goddamned coward! Or because he was afraid of what I would do to his punk ass cousin once I found out. Isn't it obvious?" Patrick was annoyed by how stupid the question was.

"Sure," Father Lydon conceded. "But you are assuming Nate was primarily interested in protecting his cousin from your wrath. Are you sure that's what it was?"

"What else could it be?" Patrick asked in exasperation.

"Why do you think Nate came to visit your mother while you were in jail and tell her what had happened?"

"Hell if I know. Probably to make her tell me after I got out, after I couldn't do anything about it," Patrick replied, rolling his eyes slightly.

"He came to ask your mom if he should tell you," Father Lydon said solemnly.

"I know she didn't tell him not to!" Patrick said, almost accusingly. If anything, his mother would have been more determined to exact revenge for PJ's death than he was.

"That's true," the priest conceded, with a hint of sadness in his voice. "In fact, she warned him you might never forgive him if he didn't tell you. But in the end, I think she was glad he didn't."

"Why?" Patrick asked in disbelief.

"What would have happened if you had found out and then acted on that information, exacting revenge on Tremont in jail?"

Patrick paused. From the moment he learned of PJ's death, he hadn't considered anything beyond exacting revenge, to discharge the terrible, toxic emotions that seemed like they would poison him if he kept them contained any longer. But as Father Lydon forced him to think about the next step, he saw it all too clearly.

"I'd still be in jail right now." It pained him to admit it, but Patrick knew it was true. In prison he had imagined a million ways that he would inflict his retribution once he found out, so many times that he could taste it.

"Exactly, my son. That's what Nate understood. He wanted to tell you, and he felt terribly guilty keeping the information from you. He went to your mother in hopes that she would urge him not to, to discharge him of the responsibility."

Somewhere in the back of his head, Patrick was aware that a kid from Dorchester a year younger than he was, whose mother had relied on food stamps to keep him fed, was somehow better at helping him think about his future than his own mother.

"Okay," Patrick said, calmer now. "I guess that makes sense."

"But there's still the matter of what your cousin was doing over there in the first place," Father Lydon said.

"I guess we'll never know," Patrick sighed.

"Well, that's not entirely true. I think you should pay a visit to your friend Walsh," Father Lydon said solemnly. "Talk to him, and then remember why Nate kept all this information from you. He wanted you to have a fresh start once you got out, and you have that. Don't let anything take that away from you."

After they returned home and he said goodbye to Father Lydon, Patrick took a shower, devoured the pancakes, eggs, and bacon his mom had cooked for him, and took a nap. His mom didn't say much, but seemed relieved that he had calmed down. He woke up in the early afternoon, and set out to visit Walsh.

When he'd first been locked up, Walsh had come to visit him every month, keeping him abreast of the news of the neighborhood, and repeatedly expressing his gratitude—in coded terms of course—for Patrick's willingness to take the heat for him. But then the visits had stopped. Then after a bit longer, Walsh had begun writing to him. But they were short, handwritten notes telling him to keep strong and assuring him he'd be out in no time and pick up right where he had left off. Patrick had sensed that there was something more than guilt that was preventing Walsh from coming to see him in person. His mother had always mumbled something evasive when he asked her.

But as soon Walsh opened the door, Patrick understood why he had stopped visiting.

"What the hell happened?" Patrick asked in horror. About a third of the left side of Walsh's face and most of his neck were brutally scarred, as if he had been caught in a house fire or tortured by a madman.

"It's a long story," Walsh sighed.

"Hey, I got time."

"Well, I gotta be at work in an hour," Walsh laughed. They walked through the living room into the kitchen, and Patrick accepted a beer. Walsh took a Coke for himself and the two returned to the front stoop and sat down. "Sean did this to me," he began simply.

"What?!" Patrick was in disbelief.

"About two years after you got locked up, Sean and I were hanging out late one night. We were getting loaded—just beer and whiskey—because you know, why not? Sean was in deep with his crew hustling everything by then, and I knew it, but I didn't really care. I had a decent job in construction, but if Sean had bigger things in mind, good for him, ya know?"

"Sure," Patrick agreed, sipping his beer. It was still dawning on him how much had happened since he'd been away. And while he had been staring at his cell wall in frustration, Walsh must have been in the hospital recovering from whatever the hell he was about to explain.

"Well, Sean started talking to me about opportunities with what he was doing, and I was listening, even though I was pretty sure I wasn't interested. My brain was fuzzy—we'd been partying for a while at that point—but it started to dawn on me that he was talking about moving coke or something, not just running numbers or whatever the hell else they were up to."

"Huh," Patrick remarked. So Sean had tried to recruit each of them at some point.

"So, even though I was halfway wasted, I could tell that Sean was asking me to do some risky shit for him, like picking up product from a source and getting it to a safe house to be cut. You know, shit that will get you arrested or killed. So I mention this to him like, 'What the hell? I am not getting involved that shit, why you asking me to be your runna man?'"

"Sean got offended, like I should have been grateful for the offer. He starts to tell me I'm just a sucker, working long hard days, and I'll never be anything in life and all that shit. And that at least PJ had the balls to go out like a man."

Those were practically the same words Sean had used the night they had fought with the Chinese kids and Patrick had been arrested, but this time Sean had alluded directly to PJ's death. Patrick felt the bile rise in his throat. He had resisted the idea that Sean's willingness to use PJ had ultimately killed him, but now it seemed so obvious.

"So of course that sobered me up right away," Walsh continued. "I mean, for years Sean had been acting like he was just as confused about how PJ died as the rest of us. So I asked him what the hell he was talking about. He tried to evade it, but eventually he had admitted that PJ had been up on Ashmont Street that night because Sean sent him. Sean had just started moving small amounts of coke.

He'd made a lot of contacts with a lot of different people—Latinos, blacks, asians, everyone—and he had had some product stolen off him by some gang bangers. He was terrified, and thought the guys he reported to would have him killed. His brilliant plan was to meet up with some new gang on the other side of Dot Ave and do the same to them, steal their dope or at least buy it for really cheap. The rumor was that this new gang didn't have a lot of muscle, but was always looking for customers who wouldn't piss off Castle Gate. So Sean was going to drive a hard bargain and sell what he got for higher, to make up for what he lost."

"Was the new gang called the Norfolk Kings?" Patrick asked.

"Yeah!" Walsh exclaimed in surprise. "How'd you know?"

"Long story," Patrick said, shaking his head. "But you finish yours first."

"Well, it would have been one thing if Sean had just wanted PJ to go with him to do the deal. I mean, you know the Kings' wouldn't have sent a man solo to meet up with a new buyer, especially if he was buying bulk. But Sean was too chicken shit to even go at all. He sent PJ on his goddamn bicycle and a backpack with only half the cash to do it by himself. Said he was going to come too with the other half but never showed!"

"So as soon as the Kings realized the deal was going south, they shot him and left?" Patrick asked, rage returning.

"Something like that. Who knows? Sean wasn't even there," Walsh said shaking his head. "Said he got pulled over or some shit, but I don't believe him. But you remember PJ was shot in the leg? Maybe they weren't even trying to kill him. But he had just lost too much blood by the time he got to the hospital."

Walsh paused, as Patrick struggled to process what he was hearing.

"Sean," Patrick said in disbelief. The four of them had been inseparable for almost 20 years. The reality of Sean's betrayal was unfathomable.

"Yeah, just like we always knew, PJ didn't ride over there for no reason. He rode over there because of Sean. So of course I lost it. I took a swing at Sean and he tried to push me. But he was so wasted and I guess I was so angry that I was getting the beat down on him. Or at least that's what it felt like for a second. So then he hit me with the bottle of whiskey. He broke the bottle and my cheekbone. Whiskey spilled all over me, and then the cigarette fell out of his mouth and lit it up."

"Shit," Patrick said. That would certainly explain the scars.

"My face went up in a second, and Sean took off scared, I guess. I screamed and ran to the kitchen and threw my head under the sink, but not before all this was done. I was in the hospital for two god-damned months."

"Why didn't you tell me?"

"What was the point?" Walsh shrugged. "You had your own prob-lems, being locked up, and you were in there because of me. It's not like you could do anything about it. Neither could I. Did you know a month after the night you got arrested Brendan McCarthy got shot in the stomach by some Asians down by Castle Island? I was tired of looking over my shoulder man, what comes around goes around!"

Patrick crushed his empty beer can with his hand, and pondered what he had just learned. So all these years, Sean had been almost as responsible for PJ's death as Tre. And he had played them all, acting like their friend, pretending to be so outraged about how Boston was changing and all that other bullshit.

"Well, we can do something about it now," Patrick said thoughtfully.

"No we can't," Walsh said, shaking his head. "Sean thinks he's gonna be the next Whitey and run his own crew. He's got half a dozen punk wannabees following him around these days. There's a bunch of cowboys out there now, nobody to answer to."

"You're kidding!" Patrick almost burst out laughing at the thought of Sean at the top of some criminal empire.

"Nope," Walsh sighed. "We'll see how long it lasts. But I'm not trying to be the guy he kills just to make an example of. I almost died trying to make it right for PJ, and if you do something, you'll just get hurt or arrested again, and you just got paroled! I don't think that's what PJ would want."

"Yeah, I guess not," Patrick agreed reluctantly. *Vengeance is mine, saith the Lord.* "Shit's gotta stop somewhere."

The two sat there in silence for a few minutes, watching the cars drive by.

"Sean will probably go down on his own," Patrick said, a hint of hope in his voice.

"Oh definitely," Walsh agreed. "Everyone's saying Whitey got tipped off by the Feds all the time. That's how he lasted as long as he did. Sean won't last six months."

"Yeah, you're right," Patrick said. "Things are definitely changing."

CHAPTER 26

March 1, 1995

*D*EAR NATE,

Just wanted to drop you line to tell you I finally got out. I did learn to type a lot better in prison, so at least I listened to that part of your advice. Are you on this e-mail thing yet? Walsh, of all people said he'd show me how, can you believe it? They have it at the library apparently. Father Lydon says no one is going to write regular letters like this anymore. We'll see, I guess.

Anyway, I'm sorry I didn't answer those letters you sent. I really do appreciate it though. I've been doing a lot of thinking, and I didn't want to write you until I'd sorted through my thoughts, if that makes sense.

I wanted to tell you that you were right about me thinking the world would just roll out the red carpet and give me what I wanted. Politics was probably never gonna happen anyway, but now I can at least focus on moving forward. I'm starting at Suffolk in the fall. Ma's helping me, but I'm going to pay her back bartending, since I'm finally old enough. I think I'm going to take business courses, and who knows? I might even buy a pub eventually. Maybe make it a chain. But one thing at a time.

Ma finally told me about Tre, or Mo. That's what we called him inside. I won't lie: I was really, really mad when I first heard. But I understand why you didn't say anything. If I'd have killed Tre in prison, I'd still be there. You were thinking ahead, like you always do. I'm going to try to do that too.

Now I need to tell you something. Someone I've known my whole life named Sean (I don't think you ever met him) was the one who made PJ go to your neighborhood. Sean lost some dope for his bosses at the time, and he sent PJ to try to pick up some more. So the whole thing is as much Sean's fault as it was Tre's. And of course PJ should've known better than to do something that stupid. But whatever. The world is screwed up. I know I don't have to tell you that.

I also wanted to say that you deserve every good thing that has happened to you. I spent a lot of time locked up in there feeling like it wasn't fair. Like that college life was mine and somehow the universe screwed up and gave it to you. But you and your ma have worked hard for every damn bit of it. I know that. I watched you do it. I just didn't understand it at the time.

The bottom line is I was just feeling sorry for myself before. I did some stupid shit. I still don't think it was as bad as what some of these people do and get away with, but that doesn't matter. I gotta take a page out of your book and focus on what I can control.

Are you coming back to Boston after college? I hope you are. I don't think I could ever leave, although I'd like to move Ma to a nicer place someday. Danielle is dating some accountant or something, so hopefully that will work out for her, and Shannon is doing really well in high school. Kiley went away to college, but she's supposed to come home for the summer in a couple months, so we'll see if that goes anywhere for me.

If you come back this way anytime soon, I hope you stop by the pub on Boylston Street for a brew or a maybe a ginger ale, if your mom is still smelling your breath every night, ha ha. I sent a letter to my *parole officer requesting to leave the state. If I am granted I may take a road trip down to Florida, don't be surprised if you see me up in the stands watching you running game on the court!*

Your Friend,
Patrick

Courtesy of the University Archives & Special Collections Department, Joseph P. Healey Library, University of Massachusetts Boston: Mosaic records

Please visit the UMass Boston exhibit
"Stark and Subtle Divisions:
A Collaborative History of Segregation in Boston"
at https://bosdesca.omeka.net/
for more information and knowledge of
Boston's Desegregation History.